UNDER HIS EMBRACE

LEONA WHITE

Copyright © 2024 by Leona White

All rights reserved.

No part of this book may be reproduced in any form or by any electronic or mechanical means, including information storage and retrieval systems, without written permission from the author, except for the use of brief quotations in a book review.

❦ Created with Vellum

ALSO BY LEONA WHITE

Mafia Bosses Series

The Irish Arrangement || The Last Vendetta

The Constella Family

Under His Protection || Under His Watch || Under His Control

BLURB

She's my past. My witness. My weakness.
Now she's back. With my son.
And a killer on her heels.

I live by the gun.
She shatters my control.

Chloe Dawson. 27. My greatest regret.
One touch. Inferno reignited.
One kiss. Years of resolve... gone.

Shadows lurk. Enemies circle.
Our dance of desire and deceit begins.

A psycho stalks her.
My son's in the crosshairs.
I must choose:

My mafia family?
Or the one I never knew existed?

In my world, love is a death sentence.
>Our passion could save us.
>Or destroy everything.

"Under His Embrace": A knockout second-chance mafia romance. Explosive reunions. Shocking revelations. A love that defies death. This isn't just another mob tale – it's a battle for redemption, family, and a future bathed in blood.

1

FRANCO

Going back to A&J's Deli wasn't how I wanted to spend my morning, but I couldn't get out of the duty to follow up with this latest incident.

I was there most of the day before, when I walked through the shot-up deli with Tony, the capo who reported to me in this district of the Constella territory. He was convinced this shooting was just one more attack from the Giovanni Family, but I knew better than to assume anything could be that cut and dry. Regardless of the fact that Stefan Giovanni had teamed up with Reaper at the Devil's Brothers MC. Those collaborators wanted to end us. It was no secret they wanted to see us to ruin, to death. Every struggle for power among syndicated crime Families included a goal of completely eradicating their rivals.

"I don't know why you *wouldn't* think Stefan was behind this," Liam Gray said as he walked through the clutter and mess the Constella soldiers were still cleaning up. A select few had gone through to take pictures and collect evidence before cleanup could begin. We operated as our own system of law, and while the process of treating this like a crime scene was similar to what the NYPD did, we were faster and kept everything in-house.

Because whoever decided to shoot up this deli owned by Dante Constella would also answer to our form of "policing".

They wouldn't get away with it—whether it was the Giovannis, the Devil's Brothers, or someone else. Dante hadn't risen to power and maintained it without making many enemies over the years. Whoever shot A&J's Deli up, killing all but one employee, would be caught and justice would prevail. *Our* brand of justice. The Constella way.

"Okay," I told the former military man who'd become our best shot. And someone more like a friend than an employee, a friend I hadn't realized I needed. "Tell me, new guy," I mocked, "why do you think this would be the work of Stefan Giovanni?"

"Because we've been hearing rumors about his trying to attack again," Liam replied. He didn't take his critical scrutiny off the deli shop space as he spoke, always *on*. "At that wedding we attended, you confirmed that rumors were running rife that Stefan was plotting something and planning to try to attack us."

I almost smiled at how easily Liam said *us*. He'd fit right in, but he wasn't only a new recruit and specialized soldier. He was also marrying into the family by proposing to Eva.

"I agree. I recall those rumors, but they might just be that—rumors, perhaps intended to throw us off."

Liam crossed his arms, surveying the damage of the cover business that wouldn't be in operation anytime soon. Probably never again. The building would be better off demolished and rebuilt as something new with all the bloodshed and destruction.

"All right. Let's say this isn't the work of the Giovannis. If they were spreading rumors to throw us off and confuse us, who would've done this?" Liam raised his brows expectantly.

"Not the MC," I replied. Blindly shooting up a place was more the bikers' style, but they would make sure we knew that they'd done it. The Devil's Brothers would want all the glory. They'd gloat in attacking the Constellas and would want to rub it in our faces. So far, they hadn't said a damn thing.

Between the two, we dealt with a lot of strife. Stefan and Reaper were the two leaders who should come to mind, but I wasn't certain that was what we were dealing with here. "Stefan has been in hiding since he tried to kidnap Nina and Tessa," I told Liam. That had happened right before Liam came into our fold. "And Reaper's dealing with your killing his connection to the governor," I reminded him. Liam had taken out their connection for immunity from the law just twenty-four hours ago, and Reaper was insanely pissed off.

"You don't think Reaper could've ordered this attack in retaliation to our killing Oscar Morelli?" he asked.

I shook my head. It was another simple assumption, but it didn't add up.

"No, man." Tony approached, slipping his phone into his pocket. He was here to help supervise, but as he was still recovering from an illness, I was in charge. "The surveillance feed shows them coming in here and firing ten minutes prior to when you took your shot at the governor's assistant."

"It can't be payback for that kill," I told Liam.

"Then who are you thinking?" he asked.

I shrugged, not wanting this to spread too far. I had my guesses and ideas, but until I had proof or clues, I didn't want to start any gossip.

"I just sent you the tracking info you requested," Tony said on his way out to speak with more soldiers out front. "The surveillance feeds tracked the car the employee took, confirming they jumped into the A&J van."

I wasn't surprised. The deli was shot up and their "company" van was missing. I'd asked for the confirmation that the sole survivor—and witness—took that van. And it seemed that I was correct in that guess.

I narrowed my eyes. "But you still can't find any employee records?"

The capo shook his head and coughed, still getting over a nasty round of pneumonia from the winter season. "No. I think it's gotta be a new hire because the paperwork hasn't been filed anywhere yet."

"Eh. That's not saying much, though." A&J's Deli was a cover business. In the basement level, drugs were packaged for distribution.

Since it was such a small shop, the legitimate business end ran with a similar under-the-table mentality. Records weren't diligently kept here. Our bookkeepers were thorough, but even from their end, they couldn't tell us who was being paid as the deli's new employee.

A very recent hire. What a shitty way to start a job.

"The cameras picked up on the employee running out the back, though." Tony coughed again. "And other cameras followed and tracked the car they jumped into to flee."

Liam furrowed his brow. "No plates or license to track?"

Tony shook his head. "No. It was a rental, tied to the family. During the day, Manny and Suzie used it for delivering meats for the deli, but at night, the crew in the basement would take the decals off and use it for delivering product."

"So it's a Constella vehicle this employee took," Liam guessed.

I nodded. "They probably figured it was the quickest escape, since the keys are always in it when it's parked out back."

"Then let's go," Liam said.

I appreciated his g0-get-'em mentality. He wasn't impatient, but I already knew that he liked to be a man of action—in action. I was the same, and that was likely a reason we got along so well and had from the beginning.

As we walked outside, I tossed him my keys. He could drive while I followed the route the Constella van had gone. "It's fortunate the employee did take the van," I told Liam as we got into my SUV. "All the vehicles are equipped with tracking."

And the route the A&J van had gone was recorded. I didn't oversee too much of what the hackers did for the family. A wickedly smart technician named Sheldon handled the cyber warfare of our organization. All I ever had to do was ask, point, and tell them what I needed to know in order to do my job.

"Convenient." Liam started the SUV and pulled out of the lot. "Lead the way."

I scrolled through the route that Tony had just sent me. When I reached the end of the route, I did a double-take and brought the phone closer to see it clearer.

Beckson? Beckson, New York?

The destination was out of the city, which wasn't surprising. If that terrified—and potentially wounded—employee wanted to get away from danger, speeding far from New York City was a logical move. I had to wonder if this survivor was a witness to the attack or complicit and wanting to hide. Either way, we had a destination, and we would get answers about this employee's involvement. If they were a witness, they'd be interrogated. If they were an accomplice, they'd also be interrogated but then disposed of.

What I wasn't expecting was the proximity to the small town I used to live in. Beckson, my stomping grounds that I never returned to after I moved into the Constella organization's properties.

My surname was Constella, but I wasn't closely related to Dante or his son, Romeo. I wasn't too close to Eva, who was Dante's niece, either. I was a distant cousin, however many times removed, but I didn't spend much time in the city with them until I officially worked for them.

"Huh." I frowned as I typed the address in for where the A&J van had stopped.

"What?" Liam asked, glancing at the navigation screen.

"Nothing. Just thinking." I wasn't about to tell him that I was thinking that the small town of Beckson, New York held a plethora of memories. Memories that I'd rather cram back into a recess of my mind to never revisit.

The day I left Beckson was the last time I allowed myself to think of *her*. Of Chloe. Of the girl who broke my heart when she decided to choose a life without me.

She was never far from my mind, always lurking there as a reminder of what I'd lost and would never have again. I did my best to avoid recalling her, but it was no easy feat to erase all thoughts and recollections of one's true love.

True *lost* love.

Bitterness crept in—again—and I sighed as I looked out the window.

"Thinking about what?" Liam prompted.

About whether Beckson has changed over the years. If Chloe's parents are still there acting like judgmental assholes. If she ever came back home since I left. If she ever misses me at all.

"Nothing," I lied again.

"Yeah, right." He huffed but didn't push for more. Another reason I befriended Liam so quickly and so well was because he wasn't stupid. He was sharp and observant, clued in to when he should drop a topic. "Now that it's just you and me in here, who are you thinking for that attack? Who do you think shot up A&J's?"

Thank you. The man deserved a medal for intuiting when to change the subject. "Donny Domino," I answered.

"Isn't he the guy from the Family that was killed?"

It happened before Liam came into the family, but we'd all filled him in on the basic facts. Stefan Giovanni partnered with Donny Domino. Donny got it into his head that he could kill the Devil's Brothers MC after lying to them, but the MC men annihilated the Domino Family. Afterward, recouping from his losses by siding with the Dominos, Stefan two-timed and was now trying to ally with the MC.

"Yeah, but some people think he's just lying low and isn't actually dead." I checked my phone, dismissing the message from another capo to stay focused on this talk with Liam. "Edward, one of Tony's best soldiers, mentioned something about the attack resembling how Donny used to operate. Without mercy and with maximum bloodshed. He was a sadistic freak."

"If anyone from this Domino Family is still around, why would they be motivated to attack a Constella business?"

I have no fucking clue. "I don't know. If any members of the Domino Family are still alive, they won't have many to rely on. The bikers damn near killed them all, and they targeted all the leaders and men. It would make more sense for Donny—or any other Domino—to fight back against their so-called former allies in the Giovanni Family or against their killers in the MC. Not us. Dante stayed out of all those deals for a reason."

Liam nodded, accepting what I said as he drove on. I appreciated having him almost like a partner. He was competent and loyal, and while he handled navigating to Beckson, I was freed up to deal with the many messages I'd received while checking over the crime scene.

I was always busy like this, the highest-ranking capo of the Constellas. But this was different, having someone at my side like Liam. I could count on him, even if he was bound to be busier soon as Eva's husband.

Everything's been changing lately. Dante meeting Nina and expecting a baby soon. They'd be married this year, I bet. Then Tessa and Romeo getting engaged. Liam and Eva.

Change would only continue to come, but I didn't count on anything drastic altering my life.

Not like that. I wouldn't be paired up with anyone. I couldn't imagine sharing my life with one woman. I wasn't looking, and I never would.

Been there, done that.

I lost my one true love years ago, and the gaping hole in my heart that Chloe left kept me unavailable to ever considering letting anyone near it again.

2

CHLOE

I never thought I would return to my hometown, especially not on the run from masked men who burst into my workplace, guns blazing.

I couldn't give myself a chance to think about any of it yet. Not the sight of my new bosses gunned down and bleeding out on the floor. Not the shattered windows and stink of smoke clinging in the air, that sulfur odor mixed with the tang of blood in a nauseating combination. As I clutched the steering wheel and sped away, still high on the adrenaline rush of facing a life-or-death scenario, I grimaced and willed my stomach to settle.

Just don't think about it. Don't think back. I wasn't in a position to ward off thoughts when it was all so fresh on my mind, but I had to focus on hiding. I could embrace the freaking-out part later.

Hide and lie low. Freak out later. This wasn't the first time I'd chanted that mantra to myself. Sadly, this wasn't my first rodeo of escaping a shitty situation. The last time I'd been this scared, though, was when I ran *away* from Beckson. The irony wasn't lost on me that I was hurrying toward it now.

My heart hammered faster as I desperately steered off the highway. The exit signs for Beckson were familiar, but it wasn't a comfortable recognition. I wasn't lured here out of any sense of belonging. Beckson was no safe haven, and I doubted I could rely on any one person or place to offer me shelter.

Yet, I had to plan on pulling off and trying to hide. To run on foot. To bunker down and keep my head low like I did at A&J's deli when the shooters rushed through. In the back of the business, I tucked under a sink and curled up tight, fearing I'd be spotted and shot. Here, in Beckson, I'd need to hide even better. Small towns weren't the best location to get lost in.

My options to survive were fading, and wasn't that the damn truth. All my life, I'd felt like I operated on a low bar of standards—just to survive. To get through one day just so I could try to give the next one my best.

But my hand was forced. I had no other options to continue getting away because this van was nearly at empty. I hadn't really considered the fuel when I climbed into the driver's seat back in the city. From downtown to Beckson, I spent all the gas in my getaway.

What the hell else could I do? That pair of men showed up at A&J's so suddenly that my new bosses, the managers, didn't have a chance to duck from the gunfire. I heard it when I was in the back and hid, near the rear exit. The gruesome bloodbath I spotted through the window into the deli's shop space had me panicked and fleeing as soon as the shooters turned their backs.

After hiding and waiting for the opportune moment, I sprinted out the back, but I didn't get far. Another man was creeping in from the alley, and I just barely had the time to dive for the rusty old van that Manny and Suzie said they used for deliveries. He fired at me without pause, shouting at me to stop. I didn't. So long as I could breathe, I'd fight to survive.

I didn't know who these men were, why they'd shoot up a local deli shop, or what they could want. Moving on autopilot and driven with the instinct to flee, I got into the van and took off.

If the tank were full, I would've left the whole damn state. I would've driven faster and further to escape the SUV that chased after me out of New York. I'd lost them a little, weaving in and out of lanes, but they always seemed to catch up. My ignorance of the city aided me. I got lost, and that was how I couldn't throw them off course—because I didn't know any course.

On the highway, though, they got slightly behind with the traffic clogged up. Once we reached the open stretch of the expressway, they were able to stay on my tail.

"Okay. It's now or never," I whispered to myself, hoping that speaking the words out loud would infuse confidence into the air, into me.

I gritted my teeth and tried to breathe as steadily as possible as I white-knuckled the steering wheel. Keeping an eye on the SUV in the rearview mirror, I waited until the last second to swerve to the right and exit. Tires squealed. My shoulder ached from how hard I yanked the steering wheel to the side. Slammed up against the driver's door, I held on the best I could to avoid rolling over.

Yes! The engine growled and protested with the rough maneuvering, but I was upright and still speeding along the ramp. I did it! I was still on the move.

I pressed harder on the gas, demanding that the van give me all it had in the reserves of its tank. It had to go. This had to work. Glancing into the mirror, I saw that I'd pulled it off. Not only did I get off the highway and not roll over, but I also lost them. The SUV didn't have enough time to get off and stay on my tail. They'd need to get off at the next exit or do a U-turn.

I bought myself time by sneaking off the expressway, but as I sped into Beckson, I winced at the noises from the van. That arrow was below E after my daring escape. No gas remained in the tank. Running on fumes, I had to think fast. Really fast.

Frantic and still so on edge from trying to run, I scanned the barren stretch of the highway roadside. Tall weeds remained despite the winter coming and going. Brown grass covered the land, not growing green yet with the lazy start to spring. Litter clumped at taller stems between the guardrail posts, but past all of that, I spotted another familiar sight.

The Beckson Motel was a rundown dump. It was ugly from years of neglect ten years ago when I left town, and it sure didn't look any better now.

It wasn't a great option, but I was stuck. I had no choice. The van slowed and then puttered to a stop on the road leading to the driveway for the highway motel.

Pushing it into the lot wouldn't make a difference. Besides, with the arrival of cold rain, I wasn't sure I could push it to a parking spot.

If I leave it on the highway, maybe that'll deter them.

I got out and hurried across the grassy field toward the motel, knowing that I was also running on fumes.

Of course, they'll guess that I'm at the motel. No other building stood around here on the outskirts of Beckson. As soon as those men turned around and got off at this exit, they'd come to the motel and hunt me down. The tree line to the west wasn't promising, not with those branches bare of leaves and coverage.

This motel was my only hope. Without a look back at the A&J van, I barreled through the door, startling the front desk clerk.

Oh, my God. "Winonna?" I asked, stunned that the crotchety old woman who ran the motel ten years ago was still manning this front desk.

She raised her brows, expressing the same disbelief that I felt. "Is that you, Chloe Dawson?" With a nasty cackle, she cracked up. "Oh, Lordy. Talk about the garbage the cat dragged in. Look at you." She laughed some more, taking glee in my soaked, disheveled appearance. Chills cut through me as I waited for her reaction to fizzle, but I'd be damned if she was waiting for an explanation.

"You bust outta town right after graduation, acting like you're all superior and better than the rest of us. And now look at you! Running back with your tail between your legs, eh?"

I exhaled a shaky breath, too cold, too scared, and too annoyed to deal with her. Facing this sort of judgment was precisely why I never thought to return, but I was out of luck.

"I need a room."

She laughed some more. "A room." Slapping the counter, she shook her head and wiped her tears. "*Here?* Oh, how the mighty have fallen."

Then she narrowed her eyes and lifted her chin. "For *you*, I'll give you a special rate. Three hundred a night."

My jaw dropped. That was insane. This one-start dump of a lodging wasn't worth half that price. We both knew she was price-gouging, likely out of spite and nothing else, but I didn't have time to haggle. I didn't have the freedom to drive somewhere else.

"Take it or leave it." She crossed her beefy arms and grinned.

You... I exhaled a sharp breath, wishing I could shout at her, but she was my only means of hiding. I had nowhere to hide outside. No other buildings were within walking distance, not with how quickly those men might come back. "Fine." I dug out the cash from my first paycheck—all cash and under the table at A&J's, not that I'd complain. After I crammed the remaining couple of bills back into my pocket, leaving me with two hundred dollars to live on for the rest of the night, I smacked the bills to the counter. "Quickly, please."

She stared at me, suspicious and probably wondering how she could get the rest of my money. "Don't you start nagging me to hurry, young lady." Taking her time, she got off the tall stool she was seated on and grabbed a card key for room four.

I didn't bother to ask for details about checking in or anything. As soon as I had the key, I'd bunker in for the night and pray that she wouldn't give away my details should those men come back.

Regardless, once I was in the room, I closed and locked the door. Barricading it for extra security wouldn't help. The small chair I pushed under the doorknob wouldn't hold up to those tall, muscled men, but it was all I had. All I could do.

Using all the thin, threadbare towels, I dried myself off the best I could and paced. Thunder shook and boomed outside, rattling the junky motel walls with such force that I feared the whole place would collapse. Between the pounding rain and hail, it was so loud that I still couldn't freak out or slow down to think at all. The soundtrack of the storm kept my senses heightened until I broke down due to sheer exhaustion.

As I fell asleep, I cried into the pillow, wondering how this could be my life. How I could never, ever win? I'd just moved to the city and started at A&J, hoping for a new start on life at twenty-seven. Now this. Killers chasing me down. My workplace shot up. The litany of woes and worries, the overwhelming sense of fear and dread, depleted my energy, and I fell asleep to the sounds of the storms.

The absence of the thunderous noise was my alarm clock all too soon. All night and into the morning, I woke at intervals throughout fitful sleep, but now, I was instantly alert.

They're back.

"Maybe she's in this one," a man said outside the thin walls of my room. The motel was nothing but a one-story, long length of crappy rooms, probably all the same, with nasty carpet and moldy ceilings. And it sounded like the men who'd shot up the deli were stomping right down the path, banging on all the doors.

"Open up," one shouted. A meaty fist banged on the door. It sounded so close, it had to be the room next to mine, number three. "Open up!" he repeated.

"Housekeeping," another man shouted, then laughed roughly at his joke.

"The whole fucking motel is empty," the first man said, then pounded his fist again. "Ain't no one in the office. No one in the rooms."

"But that van's out front," the second man argued.

I held my breath, knowing this was it. If they burst in here, I'd be caught. Without a second door to exit through, not even a single window to break out of, I was trapped.

"Well, two room keys are missing," the first man said. "If she's here, we'll find her."

I tensed, curling into a tight ball and wishing feebly that I could be invisible under the covers. Suspended in terror, every second fell too quickly. Time was running out. My life would be over, and in stark clarity, I regretted each and every one of my mistakes.

I'd never have time to correct any of them. I would never have a chance to make anything right again.

Especially not with *him*.

Shaking and silently crying in fear, I tuned out the fists banging on my door and the shouts of the two men trying to find me. Zoning out from their demands to open the door, I fervently wished that I could rectify the situation with my first love. The one person who'd truly loved me. The one man who'd ever cared. Reverting to the desperate thoughts in my mind, I numbed myself from reality, from the very real threat that I was trapped and cornered.

Franco wouldn't ever forgive me, but as I accepted that I was at death's door, that my life would be over as soon as those strong men broke into my room, I clung to the fantasy of fixing it all with him. Of apologizing for what I did. Of telling him that I loved him so badly that it ached.

I'm sorry. I'm so sorry, Franco. For all I've done. I love—

The door burst open, and I screamed at the blasts of gunfire.

3

FRANCO

"There's the van." I pointed out the A&J vehicle on the side of the road. It wasn't even *off* the road, like it broke down.

"We'll go up there, then?" Liam furrowed his brow as he looked ahead to a dump of a motel. The long, lone strip of rooms didn't look welcoming, but I supposed with the nonstop storms and rain last night, if this deli employee was seeking somewhere close to hide or stay, that dumpy lodging would be it.

"Yeah." I got my gun out, more than ready to get some damn answers. Every time I neared the prospect of fighting, of venting through violence, I could appreciate the opportunity to not think. To act without conscious thought. Going after the Constella enemies and assholes who dared to attack us was my job. But it was also my pleasure. Because when I let my darkness overrule logic, when I gave in to the temptation to be a brutal fighting machine and killer, I didn't have the energy to miss her. To think about her. To wallow in the pain of her rejection.

"Ready?" Liam asked as he parked my SUV further back, halfway between the motel and the A&J van. He grunted a laugh, noticing me prepared with my gun in hand. "Stupid question."

"Look." I pointed at the sturdy truck with tinted windows. It looked too nice and well-maintained to fit in at this motel. The only other vehicle parked in the lot was a station wagon from the seventies, with one wheel missing. It was propped up on a stack of bricks instead of a real jack, like it'd been left there to rust away forever.

"Yeah, that truck has got to be from the city," Liam agreed as he shut off the SUV.

"I bet it's the fuckers who shot up the deli and chased after the employee." Sheldon provided surveillance footage of two trucks pursuing the A&J van. While I didn't want to make assumptions, I was certain our attackers were here since the van was.

Before we exited the SUV, I took a picture of the truck in case it could be information to use later. The plates were smeared with mud and illegible, but Sheldon could try to run the vehicle registration and find an owner later.

"Let's go," I told Liam.

We reached for the door handles in sync, and like we'd been partners all our lives, we approached the rundown motel as two men in action who knew how to anticipate the other's actions. He hung back, keeping a lookout for anything toward the east, while I walked ahead and scoped out the surroundings to the west. We'd parked from a distance so the scant tree line could serve as a block. This way, we didn't have our backs completely exposed.

Two tall men stalked down the path. They rounded the corner of the long building, clearly looking for someone. Bulges at their ankles showed that they were packing. Both of them kept one hand beneath their jackets, indicating that they likely held on to a firearm. Between their hard scowls and tense expressions of being on the hunt, it was obvious we'd caught them actively on the hunt for this employee.

Why is it so important to eliminate the one witness to the shootout?

Are they trying to hide who ordered that attack?

It didn't add up. Spending all this energy to track down one witness seemed excessive. If the goal was to attack and obliterate a Constella business, they'd achieved that. A&J Deli would no longer remain after the cleanup.

Liam nodded at me as we snuck up to the men. They moved from room number three to its neighbor, number four. Behind them, coming from the side, Liam and I moved stealthily.

We didn't need to discuss a plan. It was a given that we'd split up, and in this even pairing, it'd be one of those fuckers for each of us to contain. Killing them was inevitable, but not until we got some answers.

"Open the door!" the shorter, bald one said.

"Someone has to be in there," his taller friend said. "Two keys weren't in the office and we're down to the last two rooms."

I tipped my chin at the taller one, indicating to Liam that I'd take him on. While we were too far to make out many details, I swore that tattoo up along his neck had to match the marking on one of the men we saw in the surveillance footage at A&J's. The men who shot the place up wore masks, but I was confident it had to be one of the same men.

Liam nodded, holding his gun higher as we rushed at the men. At the last second, when the shorter, stockier guy kicked the flimsy door in, the taller man turned to glare at us. He likely heard our footsteps when we reached the cracked sidewalk of the path in front of the rooms. While we were quiet, we had to hurry before they busted into this room and removed the witness.

Between these two men or the surviving witness, we *would* have our answers.

"Fuck. Go!" The tall man shoved his partner into the room at the same time he aimed his gun at us. We fired at the same time, but in the process as the two men attempted to get into the room, Liam charged for the shorter guy and I targeted the other.

We split up, both ducking from fire. I tucked behind a column holding up the leaking and cracked roof that hung over this path. Waiting until he ceased firing, I glanced at the window of room four. The curtains remained shut, but if the employee was in there, Liam would get it under control.

Rapid footsteps led away from me, and I took that as my cue to chase down the tall man who'd shot at me. He abandoned his partner, and running toward the parking lot, he skidded and slipped on the still-slick surface from last night's rains.

"Stop," I ordered, sprinting full-speed after him. He wouldn't get away, not with me hot on his heels and with the gun in my hand. Pumping my arms fast, I lacked a chance to aim at him, but once he shot shelter behind the beat-up station wagon, I lifted my firearm and pulled the trigger.

He wasn't fast enough to duck. The first bullet from my gun shattered the only window blocking him. Then the second hit him in the side.

The loud curse proved I'd gotten him where it hurt, where it would count. I couldn't kill him yet, but as I ran around the car and trained my gun on him, I saw that I'd wounded him to the point that he wouldn't run.

Blood and body matter splattered the pavement. He fell from the hit that cut through him from the right. If I didn't shatter his ribs, I would have damaged plenty of other organs and vital body parts.

Just in case he got any ideas, I shot both his legs too.

"Fuck!" he roared it to no one. Under this cold, gray sky, it was just me and him out here near the place I'd grown up. Beckson wasn't well populated, and the first signs of civilization only showed up closer to Main Street in town. Where Chloe's parents lived in a—

Dammit. Not now. This was no time to let my thoughts wander to her.

Out here off the highway, it was uninhabited and barren, save for the piece-of-shit motel that I assumed would've been torn down years ago.

"Who do you work for?" I asked, holding my gun to aim at his head.

He spat at my feet, then resumed wincing and rolling to his back. Both of his hands were covered in blood, but no matter how hard he compressed the wounds, he wouldn't live.

"Tell me who ordered you to shoot up that shop."

He groaned, not answering.

"Tell me now."

"Fuck you. I ain't telling you shit."

I narrowed my eyes at the slowly dying man. He'd bleed out soon enough, but he was with it enough to know what I was asking for. Intel. Information. Answers.

He intended to hold out on me and take those details to the grave. I wasn't shocked. I'd encountered many people who preferred to die before giving away a single piece of information. It was just my luck that he had to be one of them.

As I watched him struggle to breathe, blood spilled out of his mouth. Time was running out for him. It was running out for me, too, to get any answers. Studying him was a form of getting information, though. He wasn't as polished and cutthroat as the Giovanni soldiers. They were trained too well. They knew how this worked. If this man was someone Stefan Giovanni hired, he would've taken his gun and killed himself already. That was how Stefan expected his soldiers not to tell anyone a thing.

In the same manner, I didn't think this guy was a survivor from the Domino outfit. All the Mafia Families looked the same and held themselves in the same manner. This man wasn't from any crime family that I recognized.

His slurred speech and grungy appearance suggested he might be a member from the Devil's Brothers, but I didn't think that was correct either. He wasn't wearing a cut and he seemed slightly different from the bikers who'd been making our lives hell lately.

"I ain't telling you sh—"

I shot him, not in the mood to wait him out. He'd made up his mind not to tell me anything, and I expedited that process. I didn't have all day to wait around. Liam might have better luck in that room, and that was why I turned to rush back there and hopefully help interrogate that shorter man.

No one appeared as I sprinted back to the motel. Not a worker. No guests. Only the distant drone of vehicles speeding along the highway met my ears.

I slowed to a jog as I ran to the open door to room four.

"Dammit," I announced as I walked in.

The short, bald man was dead, lying on the ground with a bullet hole between his eyes. Liam was an expert marksman.

"He wasn't telling me anything," he replied, uninjured near the bed. "I tried, but…" He sighed and shrugged.

"Yeah. The other one didn't talk either." I furrowed my brow, assuming not all was lost. Liam stayed crouched near the bed, hovering over another body. "Is that the employee?"

"It is."

I walked closer. "Dead?"

"No. But he reached her and she knocked her head on the edge of the nightstand in the commotion before I could get him away from her."

Her. A woman.

"Knocked out cold, but she's got a steady pulse," Liam replied as I approached the prone body of a slender blonde on the disgusting carpet.

He blocked her face, but that long, blonde hair was like a sucker punch to the gut. Soft and so golden, even in lousy lighting. *Like Chloe.*

Before I could scold myself for thinking of her again, I neared them and realized it would be impossible to talk myself out of letting her stay in my mind. I blinked once, not trusting my eyes. My vision was fine, though. I stood there, stunned speechless and unable to move, shocked down to the marrow of my bone and the bottom of my heart.

What the fuck?

Confusion battled with my shock.

Because the witness, the only surviving employee at A&J's Deli, was none other than the ex I never got over.

Chloe.

It was her.

4

CHLOE

Between the sharp, stabbing pain at the back of my head and the lighter taps on my cheek, I woke up with a nasty headache. Bile rose. Dizziness rattled my bearings, and as I squinted my eyes closed tighter to avoid facing what awaited me, a low groan rolled through my chest.

Pain took over my body. After the rush from last night and at least a decade of skimping and saving to the point that I was chronically malnourished and low on energy, I didn't want to get up. I needed more rest. I wanted to sleep. I had to have five more minutes to let my body recharge.

"Get up."

I winced, more aware of the facial movement I made. The man who ordered me was firm but not mean.

Unlike the other ones who... Who...

I frowned, still lacking the energy to open my eyes. Thoughts floated out of my reach. On the edge of my conscious awareness, memories threatened to come back.

Unlike who? I was scared before I passed out, but then again, I was always terrified. How couldn't I be with the life I led, with the consequences I had to suffer from the horrible choices I'd made?

I'd been running. Again, nothing new. But this time, it was different. I couldn't run too far or too hard because I had a job. I had bosses who'd expect me to show up at my new job now.

Manny and Suzie. I worked for them. I thought I did. But as I caught on to their names, more memories rushed back in. They were dead. Shot at that deli shop. The men who killed them chased me too.

More recent, hazy images flitted through my mind's eye. I saw myself driving the A&J van. Seeing Winonna at the motel check-in desk. Hiding in the bed but falling to the carpet to hide under the bed. Then those men bursting through the door.

All the ideas seemed so far away and loose, like I was on the outside looking in. Like I was floating, untethered.

Am I dying? This numb sense of pain and weightlessness didn't make sense. I'd driven myself to the point of exhaustion before. Moving to New York and starting a new job was stressful, but to witness murders on top of it all?

Am I dead?

"Wake up," the man ordered again. His hand patted at both of my cheeks, and the slight impact jarred me again. I couldn't take solace in the darkness of unconsciousness any longer. Not with how determined he was to wake me up and jostle me.

"I..." My mouth was too dry. My throat felt tight, but as I woke up more, my lungs couldn't fill fast enough.

"Slowly," the man encouraged. "Hey," he said. "Are you all right?" His voice shifted, like he'd moved his head and spoken to someone else. If he had been asking me that question, I wouldn't have been able to confirm whether I was. This emptiness and lack of willpower worried me.

Am I dead?

I only had to open my eyes, but it was such a struggle to do so. Everything was a struggle, but I always powered through. I had to, if not for myself, then for my son.

Wrenching my eyes open was too sudden of a shift. Light penetrated and caused tears to well up. Blinking faster, I tested out more of a range of facial movements to combat my eyes tearing up at the brightness.

And once I cleared my vision to focus on the people leaning over me, I felt more confident than ever that I was dead.

I had to be.

Because the man standing to the left was none other than my biggest regret.

It can't be. It can't be him.

The man who looked like Franco was a cruel reminder of the mistake I would never be able to apologize for. *He* wasn't my regret. I hated how I'd left him and rejected his life.

I was just thinking of him, clinging to the disappointment that I would never be able to fix things between us. Those men were coming into the room to kill me, and in the clarity of the moment before my death, as my life proverbially flashed before my mind's eye, I had thought of him. I'd missed him one last time. I mourned the loss of him in my life for just one more moment.

He couldn't be here. It wasn't him. There was no way.

Unless I'm dead. And he is? And we're seeing each other in another plane of existence? Or nonexistence? My thoughts grew jumbled as I tried to latch on to what—or who—I was looking at.

"Chloe."

Oh, God. He spoke my name just like I remembered. The sound of those syllables rolling off his tongue took me back to over ten years ago. When he begged me to understand how much he loved me. That he'd never stop loving me.

"I…" I cleared my throat and tried to swallow. Where I had been parched and dry a moment ago, I was now overwhelmed with pending tears. Forcing my mouth to work, I fought past the lump of emotions clogging my throat. Speaking had to be proof that I lived. I couldn't be talking in my death. Or capable of sight.

"Franco?" I asked, still croaky but able to speak. "Is it really you?"

I felt so dumb, so bewildered, but confused.

"Fuck." He shook his head, raising his brows to complete the rest of his expression of complete shock. Looking as surprised as I felt, he made no move. He didn't budge, standing so still and staring at me intensely that I wondered if he was holding his breath in suspense.

"Oh, my God."

Too many things clicked in my mind. Fear of those men trying to kill me. Franco showing up in the wake of such grisly violence. And now, him staring down at me as I still struggled with the need to run and hide somewhere safe.

Franco. The main reason that motivated me to run from him ten years ago came back clearly. He wasn't only an ex-lover, the one man I thought I'd cherish forever.

He was a Mafia man. A killer. A ruthless individual capable of unspeakable violence.

I didn't summon him here by thinking of him as my life flashed before my eyes as I neared death. I wasn't dead and entering a phase of the afterlife.

Franco was likely here because he was connected to the deli being shot up.

Oh, my God. I feared moving to the city in case I could run into him. But the Big Apple was huge, so large that I could hide among the crowds. That was my first mistake—ever coming back close enough to where the Constella Family ran its businesses.

God, I'm so stupid. I've been so damn dumb. I had been so eager to escape and start over with a new life for me and my son, I hadn't considered how crappy the odds could be for me to see Franco or anyone from his organization.

"I... I can't do this." I struggled to get up, helped by the other man frowning at me as he held my elbow and assisted me in getting off the floor.

Dizziness swamped my mind. I blinked, lightheaded and off-kilter from being knocked out. I was hazy, but I saw how my shaky words impacted Franco.

His furrowed brow straightened. Lines dipped on his face as he shifted into scowling. That almost-stoic glower hit me hard, and as I thought back to the little I'd said, I realized what I'd done.

I told him that line before. I said those same words before I ran away from him, from Beckson.

I can't do this.

I was a strong woman. I had to be as a single mother caught in a twisted role of being a victim of something worse.

But I couldn't do this. I really couldn't. I refused to face Franco and suffer through the guilt and heartache of how we'd split. I couldn't stomach the gut-wrenching pain of knowing I'd hurt him all that time ago.

I broke his heart once. I shattered my own in doing so, and I could *not* let him get close enough to it again. I hadn't even picked up all the pieces and stitched them back together. I would need his forgiveness to come close to gluing my soul into one again.

"I can't…"

"No. Fuck that, Chloe," Franco growled.

"Do you…" The blond man volleyed his stern gaze between us. "Do you know her?"

"I can't." I shook my head, frantic to get up and bolt out of here. I ran from him once, and I had to again—now more than ever if he was involved with the shooting at my new workplace. My new former workplace.

"You're coming with us," Franco demanded, not moving out of my way.

Clumsy and shaken from all the fear, then being knocked out so suddenly, my attempt to get away was too weak to be effective. I slumped to the carpet, grimacing at the jolt of pain up my body from the drop. Stinky odors crept too close for comfort, and I scrambled to get on my hands and knees again.

"Get her, Liam," he ordered the other man.

"No. Please." I resisted Liam from grabbing my arms, but he was gentle. He guided me to stand and didn't release me as we left the nasty motel room. If he hadn't held onto my arms, I would've fallen. And if he'd taken his hands off me, I would've tried to escape anyway.

I couldn't trust Franco. Not with my heart, nor to know where he intended to take me.

I was on my own—again—but I could hang on to the fact that Caleb, my son, was safe. He would always be safe as long as he was far from Franco and everything he represented. But I couldn't assume the same for myself.

I would never repeat the mistake of thinking I could ever be safe with Franco again.

5

FRANCO

I can't believe it.

Of all the people who could've been the only surviving employee from the A&J Deli, it had to be her. Of all the people in the world. Of all the people in New York City, which sometimes seemed to be a world of its own.

It had to be her, the woman who got away from me.

Nothing could've prepared me for actually seeing her again. I spent the last ten years of my life wondering about her. She was always on my mind, whether I wanted her there or not. Thinking about Chloe had me running through a gamut of emotions—pain, anger, disdain, and loneliness. They hadn't readied me for ever seeing her again, but now that I had in one of the unlikeliest situations ever, I could reconcile my dreams of running into her with the reality facing me now.

Chloe Dawson was the employee who ran from the deli. And she would need to be questioned about her involvement there, or what she saw.

I wasn't ready to question her. First, I had to get over this shock of seeing her. Likewise, I couldn't touch her and physically keep her under my grip. If I could lay hands on her... I wasn't sure how I'd react. If I'd want to strangle her for leaving me so cruelly, if I'd want to hold her and comfort her for what happened at the shooting, or if I'd want to hug her tight and beg her to never leave me again. I wasn't sure if I'd be able to ever let her go again, because despite the despair she'd caused me, my heart had never moved on. I wasn't sure it could. My heart belonged to her, whether I wanted it to or not.

Fortunately, Liam understood that. He seemed to realize quite quickly that I knew this woman and that she was personally aware of who I was. Without my needing to explain a thing, he intuited that he had to take charge for me here. While he handled her, I took the time to try to adjust and get over the shock. It crippled me, and I needed more time to feel like I could handle this how I was expected to as the highest-ranking capo of the Constella Family.

"Franco," Andy, one of our loyal soldiers, said as he approached.

Liam guided Chloe out the room, and I trailed behind him, taking the chance to really rake my gaze over her to better know that she was here, in my life, not a dream or memory. Her golden locks fell over her shoulders, and those gray-blue eyes were the same captivating orbs that sucked me in as they had before. She was always tall and athletic, very slender and trim, but she had aged into more of a womanly figure over the years with curves to make her all the more enticing.

I nodded at Andy, tearing my gaze from Chloe. I'd asked a crew to follow Liam and me out here, but they'd taken a little longer to arrive.

Thank fuck you're here now.

"Take..." I sighed, catching myself from uttering her name.

"Take the witness," Liam instructed as he handed her over to Andy and the other Constella soldier who'd arrived with him.

"Yes, sir," Andy said, showing no issue with deferring to Liam regardless of how long he'd been working for us. All of them understood that I'd delegated Liam to a higher status from the beginning.

As Andy maneuvered Chloe toward the SUV he'd come in, I tore my stare from her and focused on getting back into my car to resist the temptation of looking at her. She wasn't going anywhere. She was in our custody, and while Andy drove her back to the Constella properties in the city, Liam and I would follow behind them.

Once we were in the car, I exhaled the full breath that I'd been holding in. Now that I was out of her presence, I could try to steady myself—and prepare to face her again. Seeing her was such a physical hit that I had to work through the stress of such a surprise.

There weren't many things that could render me feeling like a rug had been swept out from beneath my feet, but encountering Chloe did.

Liam cleared his throat as he started the car and pulled up to tail the other SUV Chloe rode in. "The man I killed in there didn't say a word."

Thank you. I appreciated his changing the subject and not bombarding me with questions about how I reacted to seeing Chloe. He was curious. He had to be, but he wasn't pushing.

"Neither did the man I chased down. He wanted to take his intel to the grave."

Liam nodded. "I don't have much experience to make this call, but they didn't seem like Giovanni soldiers."

"No, I don't think they're Stefan's soldiers." I frowned, staring at the SUV in front of us, knowing it wasn't just any ordinary car but one that held the woman I once loved. "Nor do I think they were bikers from the Devil's Brothers MC."

"Agreed. They could be independent contractors, too."

I nodded. "Let's say they were. Who hired them to hit us?"

Liam shrugged. "I'm not sure. I haven't been here long enough to know."

He had a good point. "And it didn't look like anyone from the Domino Family, either."

"Which means it'll be interesting to hear what this eyewitness can tell us, that new employee who escaped." He glanced at me. "Will you be able to question her?"

I rubbed my forehead, feeling the start of a tension headache creeping in. "I will." A bitter grunt escaped me. "When it comes to

Chloe, it seems that she will be a living reminder of how I'll always do my duty above all else."

"What does that mean?"

It means I was torn from her because of my job once. And I bet it will forever stand between us.

"Who is she? Come on, man. Talk to me. I'll try to help. If you can't handle being near her, then I'll step up where I can. But don't keep me in the dark."

Eva and Romeo were aware of how she broke my heart. Dante wasn't ignorant either, but when it happened, he'd been too busy to get too involved with checking on me.

"That woman was the sweet girl I fell in love with when we were teenagers. We both grew up in Beckson, and we were together in high school." *Junior high, too.* "She was my life, but as I got older, I knew that I would be expected to move to the city and work for Dante. I knew that I was expected to get busier with more official roles for Dante in the heart of the organization, just like Romeo was."

"But you didn't grow up near Dante and the others?"

I shook my head. "My mother wanted to be closer to her sister-in-law, my aunt, who was in long-term care here. I lived with her since my father died, but it was understood that I was always a part of the Constella organization."

"Okay. Then what happened?"

She ran.

I zoned out for a second, watching the SUV ahead of us, knowing her days of running were over for now. We wouldn't let her go until we were finished with her.

"I wanted her to come with me to the city, but her parents were against it."

Liam huffed. "What, they didn't approve?"

"No. Not at all. Judge and Mrs. Dawson were self-righteous pricks who did not ever approve of their only daughter dating someone like me, affiliated with the Mafia. She was always arguing with them, insisting that we loved each other and that we should have the chance to be together after she graduated high school. I was done already, just waiting for her to come with me to the city. I came back every weekend to be with her when I was training with Dante and the soldiers in the city. I promised to bring her with me, away from her parents, but she was too scared of their control and displeasing them.

"Instead, she ran. She took off and I never heard from her again. She had a few scholarships to consider, but I don't know where she went. The day I begged her to consider coming to the city with me, she told me she couldn't do it. Then she was gone. She didn't choose me."

Afterward, I reacted poorly. I immediately shifted to a life of sleeping around and being the ultimate playboy. Flings and one-night stands were supposed to erase the grip she had on me, but it never made a difference. I belonged to her, even though she discarded me and the love we shared. No woman ever compared to her, and she was the measuring stick I held everyone else to. A lifetime of sleeping around couldn't remove her from my mind. The memories of her lingered until this day.

"Damn."

I grunted a wry laugh. "Yeah. That sums it up."

"Then how—or why—did she end up working for a Constella business?"

"I doubt she planned it like this. My guess is that she didn't know A&J Deli *was* a Constella front business. If she did, she'd keep a wide berth. Her parents poisoned her to think all of us in the Constella Family are nothing but evil."

"Well, she was clearly there when the shooting happened. And she might have answers."

"About her job there," I said. *But not about why she left me. Why she stomped on my heart and rejected the connection we had.*

"I can question her," he offered. "If it's too much to face her again."

"No." I shook my head as the SUV she rode in pulled into the driveway. We'd brought her to the empty house next to the mansion where Dante lived with Nina. The adjacent building wasn't vacant, but no one currently lived there, which made it an ideal middle ground for anything we might not want to bring to Dante's home.

"You sure?" Liam asked.

I nodded. I wasn't sure. I was far from ready to speak with Chloe. I was eager to get answers, to do my job and follow up with the one witness to the shooting. I had to do my job and see to my duty. At the same time, I was burning with curiosity and the urge to demand an answer for how she'd treated me in the past. An explanation for how she could tell me that she'd love me forever, but in the next moment, turn around and tell me that she couldn't do this with me anymore.

"Yes. I'll handle it." I had to. Facing my ex who still held my heart wouldn't undermine my commitment to my job.

We exited the cars, and with Liam, I stood at the back door to where Chloe would step out. When she did, she faltered in her step.

"Are you all right?" I caught myself from reaching out to steady her. Liam glanced at me as he held her by the elbow.

Dammit. I could not let her see how she still got to me. I couldn't let her see how much this had thrown me.

"Are you injured?" I asked instead, leaning on the clinical, factual manner of that question.

"No. Just from knocking my head," she mumbled as she rubbed the spot.

"Get her food and water," I instructed a guard at the house, no longer able to look at her. It was too hard. I warred with the battle of wanting to hold her and scold her. She had me twisted up, and seeing her so vulnerable and intimidated…

"What about Danicia?" Liam asked, referencing the former ER doctor who worked for the family.

I nodded. "Yes, just to make sure her head wound won't be an issue."

"Don't talk about me as if I'm not here," she snapped.

I faced her, hardening myself from caring. From worrying. I didn't last long. I couldn't look at her and forget about all the pain she'd caused me. She'd wounded me. She broke my heart, and I wasn't sure I could turn the other cheek and handle facing her, no matter how long ago it was that she'd rejected our love.

"What's this?" Romeo asked as he walked out of the house, barely having a chance to look at Chloe as the guards took her inside. She hung her head, not brave enough to lift her face.

"The eyewitness from the deli," Liam answered as I fell under the spell of wanting to go after her. I couldn't look away, stuck with the loss of her walking further from me. I was damned to look at her and damned if I didn't.

"Oh?" Romeo glanced at her and then me, furrowing his brow. "What's wrong?"

I huffed. *So much that I can't begin to cope.* "It's Chloe Dawson."

He looked back toward her, then did a double-take. "Isn't that the name of the girl who—"

"Yeah." I shook my head and turned. "You can question her. I need a moment to process this."

A minute wouldn't be enough to process the whirlwind of seeing the woman I loved and lost again.

I already spent half of my life missing her. And I wasn't sure if this reunion could be a blessing of having her close to love again… or damnation that could set me free once, and for all.

6

CHLOE

They caught me. Franco's Mafia men had me in this car and they wouldn't let me go. I didn't ask. I didn't waste my breath begging for them to release me, either.

If the Constella Mafia was involved in the deli shooting, they would take the incident into their hands. No one would dare to question them. None of them would contact the police—including me. I intended to stay under the radar of the "real" law and authority, but I sure as hell hadn't anticipated ending up under custody of this unofficial branch of justice.

Of all Mafia Families, I had to get mixed up with his?

I went from running from gun-toting strangers to winding up in the backseat of this SUV. I struggled to accept how this was my life, that all that I'd done had ended me up here, but I knew better than to think of a way out of it.

I wasn't a stranger to the Mafia. Franco had always known he'd serve as a soldier for his uncle's organization. He never kept it a secret when we dated, and he never got mad when I asked questions about how it all worked. Details weren't given, and I never outright asked for specifics that would compromise my safety. I wasn't stupid, only dumb enough to fall in love with him, the bad boy my parents disapproved of so vehemently.

Seeing him was a shocker, but I couldn't lower my guard around him. In that first look we'd shared in that motel room, through surprise at seeing each other, I felt so much weight in his gaze. Too many heavy things passed between us, all the unspoken but powerful feelings that neither of us could deny. Franco and I had volumes of history, but that couldn't matter now. It couldn't be relevant with why they captured me.

No. Wait. Franco and Liam hadn't only captured me. They'd also saved me. I spotted the dead man who'd been chasing after me since shooting up the deli. If not for Franco and Liam, I would've been dead. Caleb would've been an orphan.

In this light, Franco was my hero, but I'd be damned if I'd let that get in my head. He was a Mafia henchman, a man who chose a life of crime and corruption—both things he claimed fell in the line of "duty" to his family.

I had to remain on guard, no matter how much I yearned to see him again in other ways. In the way that he so easily reminded me of our youth, when we were young and so in love.

When we parked at a huge complex of enormous houses, I struggled to make eye contact with him. While I felt every tense bit of pressure when he stared at me, I couldn't face him. Not with all these men. Not in a public setting like this. While the men spoke, I tried to look around and figure out where they'd taken me.

"Are you all right?" he asked.

I watched as he reached out his hand to steady me, but he seemed to think twice as he lowered his arm.

In what universe could I be all right after running into you, Franco?

"Are you injured?" he asked instead.

"No. Just from knocking my head," I muttered and gently probed at the spot.

"Get her food and water," he ordered.

"What about Danicia?" Liam asked.

Who?

"Yes, just to make sure her head wound won't be an issue," Franco replied.

And if it is an issue, it's my issue! "Don't talk about me as if I'm not here."

"This way," a guard instructed, gesturing for me to proceed toward the house. After snapping at Franco, I couldn't dare to glance at him. For all I knew, he was counting down the time until I wouldn't be here. I hadn't committed a crime to work at A&J's Deli. Nor had I done anything wrong in trying to run and hide from those killers. They had no right to treat me like I was an accomplice or an instigator of more trouble.

It's not like they're binding me up. It was a small grace, but I had to appreciate it.

They ushered me inside to a room and closed the door. As soon as the guards had left, another returned with a tray of food. This guy didn't say anything, either. He set the food and bottle of water on a table, and only then did I slump to the edge of the bed and sigh.

My God. This is a disaster. I rubbed my face, overwhelmed with all the chaos, but deep down, I was grateful that it was just me suffering this time. With Caleb on spring break, he was far from this danger. He was staying with a friend in Brooklyn who lived with his grandpa, and I was so damn happy that I didn't have to worry about him here as I settled into a new job.

What job?

I shook my head. While I hadn't known Manny and Suzie at the deli for long, I did miss them and what they represented. They were supposed to be my new employers, bosses who wouldn't mind paying me under the table and keeping things on the down-low. Regardless of how well I could've gotten to know them, I was certain they were innocent and didn't deserve to die like that.

Now, my new start on life would need to be restarted again.

As soon as I get out of here.

I glanced up at the door as someone knocked, then entered. The tall man wasn't the one I both dreaded and looked forward to seeing again. It wasn't Franco, but his distant cousin.

"Romeo?" I guessed. That was the name of the man he referenced the most, Romeo, the son of Dante—the Boss.

"Yeah." He laughed once, lightly. "I'm surprised you remember."

I nodded and cleared my throat. "Franco mentioned you. Way back when."

"Right." Romeo took a chair and turned it around to straddle it as he faced me. "Long time ago. It's definitely a surprise to see you again —like this."

Like what, though? Romeo was settling in to chat, and it was with a heavy stomach of discomfort that I realized he'd be asking me questions. Franco seemed to want nothing to do with me.

And how can I blame him, anyway?

"Chloe?"

I blinked, jarred from my musings. "Where's Franco?"

Romeo shrugged. "Busy. So, tell me. How come we're experiencing this blast from the past, reuniting like this?"

I heaved in a deep breath, almost grateful for the chance to talk about this. Ever since those men came into the deli, I'd been bottling it all up. "I reported to A&J's for my shift, but ten minutes into it, two men burst in from the front door and started shooting the place up. I dropped in the back storage area and hid. I had no clue what was going on. I was so terrified, I froze and balled up, hoping I would stay out of sight."

"Did you recognize them?"

I shook my head and described what I could. "They wore masks, too. From where I sat, I couldn't see too much of the shop floor, but I saw Manny and Suzie on the—" My throat tightened at the flashback.

Romeo uncapped the water bottle and offered it to me. "Go at your own pace."

I nodded, then sipped the offered water. "They were dead, lying in all that blood on the floor."

"Did they say anything?"

I frowned. "Manny and Suzie? No, they didn't have a chance to do more than scream."

"I meant the shooters."

"No. If they spoke to each other, I didn't hear it over the gunfire. As soon as I heard them, I hid."

He sighed. "Then what?"

"I slipped out the back, thinking I could just run. I walked to work—I mean, so far. I only moved to the city a couple of weeks ago and happened to buy a couple of things in the deli when Manny said they were looking to hire some help." I shrugged. It was strange how that felt like ages ago but had only happened two weeks in the past.

"As soon as I got outside, another man appeared—another one in a mask—and he shot at me. I dove for the van and just focused on getting the hell out of there. The next thing I know, they were chasing me in that truck. I got lost in the city, which kind of helped to lose them, but they caught up to me on the highway. The van was about to lose gas near Beckson, so I swerved to get off the ramp there and hid in that nasty motel room. I didn't know where else to go. I didn't have my phone or money or anything." *I hate reliving this.* "I was so exhausted that I passed out. But they came back. I don't know why they waited all night, maybe the rain, but they searched the motel and I knew I was cornered. But then Liam and Franco were there and..."

"And they took care of those men." He asked a few more questions about the shooting, but I didn't have anything else to add. I didn't know anything. It happened so suddenly, and I'd only been working there for so long.

"What about—" Romeo stopped speaking when Franco entered the room.

I sat up, taking note of his stern demeanor as he stalked in. "I can handle it from here." He set his hand on Romeo's back. The tall, tatted man nodded, then stood.

"You sure?" Romeo glanced back at me.

"Yeah. All recorded." Franco sat and nodded at the phone recording the audio of this conversation.

"Okay. I'll wait to speak with you afterward," Romeo told him.

"Drink that water," he advised me as he headed for the door. "You look dehydrated."

No, just tired. Of life. Of struggling. Of all of it. But I dutifully showed him the bottle then took a sip. It served as a prop, at any rate.

Franco wasn't going to let anything stop him from asking me questions. He must have been listening to what I told Romeo because he didn't start with the shooting. He went further back.

"Why were you working at that deli?" His tone was firm, mad, even, and I didn't want to decipher why he'd be angry at me. I was the victim here.

"I didn't know it was associated with your family."

"That's not what I asked."

I narrowed my eyes, hating that he'd be this confrontational. Then again, with the way I left him, why wouldn't he be? "I wanted a job that paid under the table."

"Why?"

I shook my head. "My personal life isn't your business." *Not anymore.*

He huffed. "Yeah, you've made *that* clear. How did you end up at A&J's? Walk me through it, from the moment you left Beckson to now."

I bristled. "I just told you that my life isn't your business."

"The sole surviving employee of a Constella-owned business is. The life of the eyewitness to an attack on a Constella-owned business is. So fill in the details, Chloe. Explain to me how you're not involved with this shooting."

You asshole.

"What happened since you told me that you 'can't do this' all those years ago and left me?"

Oh, Franco. My heart softened at his hurt tone, but I couldn't press rewind and undo the damage I'd done to him. "I went to college in New Mexico, on a scholarship. I dated a few guys. I ended up dropping out when my courses got too hard with maintaining other things."

"What other things?"

I ground my teeth slightly, damning him for picking for details. "Hobbies. Family."

He rolled his eyes at that mention. I didn't mean family as in my judgmental parents I couldn't stand, but *my* family. The very small one I'd started.

"I mainly just worked hard at whatever jobs I could find and tried to avoid contact with my parents. They were too overbearing." *And still are.*

"That's it? That's all that you've been up to since you left town? All that happened between when you left me in Beckson and your showing up to work at A&J's?"

I nodded, praying he'd buy it.

He stared at me, seeming to search my face for any clues of deception. I wasn't in the mood to tell him my biggest secret. The longer I kept that sliver of truth in my mouth, unspoken, the more he seemed to get angry.

There was no way this sexy man could be a mind reader and just *know* that I wasn't telling him all of it.

"Was it worth it?"

"What?" I held my breath, suspended on the edge of nervousness and confusion.

"Was it worth it? All those years that we were apart. Was it worth it?" His lips stayed pressed in a firm line. As he leaned over, his blond hair shaded his brow. Slanted closer, he seemed stuck in a struggle not to reach out to me. He refrained, but the tension between us grew and grew.

I stared at him, refusing to answer. "It's not fair of you to put me on the spot like that. Now? After I was chased and nearly shot down and..." I growled, shaking my head. "You can't ask me that out of the blue. You wouldn't have understood my reasoning. Not then or now." I stood, too upset and intimidated to sit here and take this line of questioning that had nothing to do with what his Mafia family could care about. My reasons to leave him had nothing to do with the deli shooting.

"It's not fair of you to still be so mad now," I insisted.

"No." He shot to his feet and stepped closer. "No, Chloe. It's not fair that I've spent half of my life missing you."

I frowned, bothered about his troubled expression and stormy gaze because I was the cause of it. I'd caused him all this pain and heartache.

"Nothing's fucking fair about how you left me."

Tears burned behind my lids, but before I could will them back, he closed the distance between us and kissed me hard.

7

FRANCO

The second I crushed my lips against hers, I was consumed with deeper longing than I'd ever felt before. I thought I'd yearned for her before, all those years I couldn't get over her. I assumed I was at the bottom of despair in recalling all the memories of her when I lay in bed at night unable to sleep.

That was nothing. Now that I had a chance to savor her warm lips, parting in a gasp against mine, all my desire and grief coalesced into something so potent and intense that I was immediately sucked into such lust that I could barely breathe.

She couldn't, either. Not with how firmly I held her to me. Inhaling through my nose, I struggled against the need for air as I smashed our mouths together in wet, hot perfection.

Just like before. She was *just* like before, and the familiarity of kissing the one woman I'd always wanted left me shaken and busted apart.

I'd dreamed of this moment. I fantasized about tasting her sassy lips again. Never had I counted on having the chance to even touch her. But I was now, and I embraced it all. The zinging spark of contact between my skin and hers as I slid my hand along her jaw until I cupped the back of her head. All those glossy strands of gold whispering over my fingers so softly. The scent of her—still so sweet and vanilla. Her taste, that bold, addictive flavor of lost love.

She moaned so slightly, so quietly, in response. It was music to my ears, a sexy sound that never sounded as sexy as it did when she released it. A drugging mewl that turned me on even faster.

Too soon, she wrenched free. She pulled back and panted, staring at me with unbridled lust but also weariness in her eyes. "No." The tip of her tongue traced over her lips. "No, Franco. I shouldn't just—"

I growled, shaking my head as I dove in again. Silencing her with a deeper kiss, I waited for her to try to push me away. When she didn't, I became stuck on goading her to dare to do it again. To reject me. To give me another demonstration of how wrong I had to be about her.

But she didn't. She kissed me back, sliding her tongue out to duel with mine. She caressed my chest, running her hands up my torso until she could snake her arms over my shoulders and cling to me.

Shouldn't what, Chloe? Break my heart?

I gripped her shirt, slipping my hands under the material to torture myself with another trip down memory lane. I smoothed my fingers and palms over that soft flesh, reacclimating to the warmth of her athletic body. She had more substance to her now, more curves to hold on to.

Shoving her shirt up, I waited for her to tell me no or to protest. I anticipated that she'd halt my needy exploration that was past due for the last decade. I counted on her to flinch and recoil, to double down with a refusal of intimacy.

But again, she didn't. Instead, she slanted into me, lifting her arms so I could tug her clothes up and over her head. I ripped the fabric off and let it fall, and in the same motion, I yanked at my shirt. Buttons flew, but I didn't care. Nothing could matter except getting my hands on her again. The drive to feel her bare and flush was overwhelming, and I didn't stop until I was shirtless like her. Until her breasts spilled free from her bra. Her hard, beaded nipples poked at my chest, and the firm points elicited another growl from my lips.

"You shouldn't *what*, Chloe?" I demanded as I kissed down her jaw to reach her neck. My hands weren't idle. As she threaded her fingers through my hair and held on tight, she kept my face right at her breasts as I lowered to suckle at her generous tits.

Her pants didn't take long to unbutton, either. Once I had them off, along with her panties in this mad, rushed race to get her naked, I picked her up. Each ass cheek filled my hands perfectly. Back then, she was so slim and fit, muscular from running track and playing basketball. Now, she had more meat on her bones, and I couldn't get enough of it. Of her. Chloe tormented me in the memories I couldn't let go of and in the present moment of relearning her body again.

"You shouldn't do what?" I demanded again. Holding her up gave her the freedom to wrap her legs around my waist. At this level, I could devote my mouth to kissing, licking, and sucking on her breasts. Her nipples couldn't get any harder, jutting out at me for one taste after another. Still, I wanted her to shove me away. To push me back. To reject me—again—and maybe this time, it would fucking sink in as a final declaration that we couldn't belong together.

"I—oh, Franco." She panted, framing my face to tip my head up. I surrendered to her request, lifting my mouth to hers to kiss with abandon. She sucked on my tongue, and the tease went straight to my hard dick. But when she moaned into my mouth and cinched her arms around my neck in an even tighter hug, I swore my head would splinter apart and never get stitched whole the way it should be.

This woman gutted me. She also fired me up in all the ways that mattered—body, mind, and soul. Here and now, though, she bewitched me and taunted me to fuck her.

Lowering to the bed, I let her fall onto the mattress before me. I only carved the distance between us for a moment. I followed her down, but paused to unzip and shove at my pants.

Her legs parted for me, widening to let me settle over her. I couldn't without a good, long look over her, and I did. Taking in the view of her luscious body showed how she'd matured, how she'd changed in the last ten years, and all I could see was how she'd gotten more beautiful, more alluring, and so sensual as she gazed up at me with impatience bright in her eyes.

I hovered over her, dipping down. This was fast. This was an instant combustion of two halves of a soul fitting back together, and the mere idea of having her again made me delirious with desire. It was a force I couldn't try to control, and when she put her hands on my face to urge me to crawl up over her, I was beholden to her wishes.

"You shouldn't want this?" I taunted, still daring her to complete her blurted sentence. If she pushed me back, if she fucking said no, I had to give her up once and for all. I had to *know*. She had to tell me that there would be no possible hope. Until she severed this connection that tugged me closer and closer to her, I couldn't retreat. I couldn't rein in this boiling need to have her.

We kissed, hot and quick, before I could tease her any further and before she could reply. In the far recesses of my mind, I wanted to convince myself that her kiss *was* her answer. That in slinging her arms over my shoulders and lifting her legs to wrap around my waist, she was showing me her answer.

Fuck me. Fuck you. Fuck! I couldn't think straight, drowning in the sense of tasting and feeling this woman. The burn of contact threaded through my skin. Her presence, so warm and familiar despite the years, seeped into me and I refused to let it fade for one second.

I slid my hand lower, stroking over her pussy and spreading the copious cream leaking from her entrance. She was aroused, so wet and needy for me. I felt it in the suction of her tight entrance when I pushed my finger in. I heard it in the breathy exhale she let out at my invasive touch.

Still, she didn't protest.

Damn you. She could reject me and run. All those years ago, she chose a life without me in it at all. And now, this encounter that wavered between kismet and a curse, she was able to choose me again? To opt for more with me, a sampling of the intimacy we had when we burned up the sheets when we were younger?

"You shouldn't want me?" I growled, wishing my anger at her could trump my feral desire for her.

I angled my dick to her pussy. She didn't tense. She didn't stall me and insist on any more foreplay. Instead, she let her legs drop. Her knees slid to the sides and higher, lifting her pelvis to me. The angle was like an offering of her cunt, and I wasn't going to hesitate.

After I notched my cockhead at her slippery opening, I pushed in. The first stretch was glorious, that tight glove on my dick. It wasn't enough, far from it. With all the longing I'd endured and how much I'd missed her over the last ten years, I suffered a moment of needing to know this was real. That she was here, with me and in the flesh. To be aware that this wasn't another dream or projecting the idea of her on another woman while I wished my true love were welcoming me in.

"Franco. My God. Please." She clawed at my back as she tossed her head back. Golden strands splayed on out the pillow like a halo. But she couldn't be my angel. She was the devil, the wicked woman who broke my heart by leaving after she'd promised she wouldn't and couldn't. She ruined me by swearing that our love would stand up no matter what.

She wasn't telling me no. She wasn't rejecting me at all. I received the opposite from her. She *begged*. She urged me to slam in.

Gritting my teeth, I damned her for ever leaving in the first place. I thrust all the way into her slick, tight heat, settling myself in as far as I could go. My entire throbbing cock was in her. I was balls-deep in Chloe's pussy, and if I wasn't feeling the exquisite pressure of being sheathed so perfectly by this woman, I wouldn't have known what to make of this.

"Oh…" she moaned, low and long and dirty, and I lost it.

I wouldn't be hearing a single protest from her lips. She wasn't going to change her mind and choose to run from me now.

Not until I fucked her hard and fast, on a race to show her all that she—that we—had been missing for the last ten years. All that wasted time, gone and never to be reclaimed.

Like a machine, I pounded into her pussy, making sure to rub up against her clit with every downstroke. Then I pulled out to pummel her again.

Sweat dripped from my brow with the strain of slamming into her.

Rubbing all up over her, I pushed her into the mattress and vented all the pent-up longing I'd bottled in for too damn long.

She wasn't any stronger than me. She couldn't resist how we drew to each other, not even in this. I predicted how close she was to coming, feeling her tensing up, and she started to rock up into me and meet me thrust for thrust.

I was so close, so damn ready to explode into her. There was no chance of either of us lasting, not with how suddenly and hungrily we'd crashed after arguing. It was torture to hear her talking about a life away from me, how she'd taken off to be without me for years.

Feeling her pussy clench erased the sting of that knowledge. Letting her cry out at the intensity of her orgasm droned out the negativity in my mind that she hadn't ever reached out to me.

With another thrust in, my balls tightened and I felt my pending orgasm get closer. A tingle charged me from the base of my spine, and I was too far gone to try to savor this moment or drag out the tension of impending pleasure.

I couldn't last. Groaning loudly, I emptied into her. My dick twitched, sunken in her warm pussy that milked me good. All my cum flooded into her, just where it fucking belonged. Where it should've belonged every day for the last decade.

Stop. Stop holding on to the past. My mental scoldings were feeble, too weak to register. Thoughts ceased. Ideas faded. I could only slump down to her and relish the feeling of our chests heaving against each other. We both raced to catch our breath. Sweat slicked our skin together, and as we lay there entwined, so deeply connected like we used to be, I let my mind blank.

Until something changed. She kept her arms around me, hugging me loosely, but her body moved differently. No longer drawing in desperate pulls of air to steady herself and relax, her chest lifted against mine. With sobbing, juddering pushes, she cried.

If there were any reaction I ever could have looked forward to after fucking my ex so hard and fast without any semblance of control, this wasn't it.

I'd made her fucking cry. I wouldn't—and couldn't—take back the moment of having sex with her like this, but as I pulled out of her and eased away from her naked, flushed body, I felt like a monster.

8

CHLOE

No! Don't. Please don't leave me.

I wiped at my eyes, fighting through the blurry vision from my tears. Watching Franco get off the bed wasn't easy. I struggled with the clawing need to beg him to stay with me, to lie with me for just another moment, but that was too cruel of a request to make. I had no right to ask him to cuddle. I had no grounds to demand more tender touches.

Nothing about that quickie was tender. Half the time, he taunted me, pushing me to tell him to go away.

I hadn't been able to utter a protest once he laid his hands on me and burned up my skin. Words failed me when he explored, readjusting to loving my body.

When he first kissed me, I wanted to tell him that I shouldn't rush into anything with him until he explained why I mattered in the deli getting shot up. Or how he thought falling into bed could be wise in the context of how we'd been reunited.

"Where—" My voice was too croaky, but I fought to speak again. "Where are you going?" Sitting upright, I could track where he moved in the room. While these damn tears continued to build up and spill, I followed his movements as he retrieved his pants and shoved them on before pacing.

He didn't leave the room, and as I caught my breath, I tried to cling to that fact. He wasn't running out of here, determined to flee.

That's my job. I was the one who ran.

I caught my breath, working through the emotions that clogged my throat. It was just so much to get past. So much to endure and accept.

Now that the last waves of bliss faded from that orgasm, I was vulnerable to feel so much more than the undeniable desire and urgency to come with him.

Shock. I was rooted in a deep pit of shock and stunned marvel that I'd just had sex with the one man I'd always loved. Franco had always been the one. From the first time we kissed, I knew he was the man who would hold my heart forever.

The moment he kissed me after his heartbroken statement, that it wasn't fair of me to have left him, I felt like I had come home. Touching him, kissing him, and having him thrust into me hard like that, I *was* home. Falling into bed with Franco was living proof that I was a fool to separate from him. With him, I slotted into where I belonged in life—with him.

But that's impossible. It was too difficult to figure out back then, when I ran from home, and it was still too challenging to accept now. Our decisions had pulled us apart, and I felt disillusioned to think we could have a future together. No matter how right it felt to really be with him, it couldn't be feasible.

I heaved out one last sigh, comforted by his staying in here. He didn't leave. Pacing back and forth, steadily, as though the movement calmed him, he remained in the room, almost as though he was waiting for me to get over myself, to settle down and be able to talk.

I licked my lips, torn with the need to speak up, but I didn't know how to start or what to say.

I'm so sorry that I ran?

Please fuck me again because it makes me feel better?

Don't hate me, but can I please leave again?

Nothing would work. They were all lame platitudes that wouldn't help this situation.

"I'm sorry."

I blinked at his simple words, direct, blunt, and sincere. He wasn't talking out of his ass, but I didn't understand how he thought *he* should be the one apologizing here.

"I'm sorry I was so…" He scowled, seeming mad and disappointed with himself as he gestured at me. "I'm sorry I was so rough."

I wiped the last of my tears away and fought the hysterical urge to laugh. "Too *rough?*" It was just right. Perfect. So good that I wanted him again despite all the reasons I definitely shouldn't.

"I shouldn't have been that hard and—"

I swung my legs off the bed. "Franco, it's…" I couldn't say it was all right. If I was reduced to tears, so blindsided by how good it felt to have him deep inside me and kissing me so possessively again, nothing was all right.

"Come here." He held out his hand, helping me stand. Once I was on my feet, he pulled me into a tender hug. It wasn't an excuse to cop a feel, but an embrace of security. "Let me at least clean you up."

I smiled, touched that he could be so soft and careful with me. Maybe that was it. He spent so much of his anger and frustration with so-called rough sex that he only had the energy to be delicate and tender now.

He led me to the bathroom, and after he turned on the water, I followed him into the stall. Hot water pounded down and massaged my body. It felt so good that I couldn't hold in a moan of pleasure. I never had a luxury like this, only affording lousy apartments with pathetic bathrooms and even lousier water tank pressure.

"See?" he said, slightly teasing. "I was too rough with you."

I smirked, keeping my eyes closed as I lifted my face to the spray of water. "Not too rough."

He rubbed his thumb over the marks he had left on me from taking me so hard. "I didn't expect to do that."

I nodded. "Me neither."

He grunted a laugh. "What do you mean?"

"Well. Seeing that you killed that man who was chasing after me, I think it's not farfetched to think that you and Liam saved me back there. And that what we did in the other room could be mistaken as some weird form of gratitude."

He cleaned up, letting me start on my head. This was the first time I could clean up since the A&J Deli shift that I never finished, and I wanted to purr at the chance to do so. I hated that I felt like I was washing away the evidence of what Franco and I did, but with him in the shower, cleaning up alongside me, I didn't suffer his absence.

"I meant that I didn't come into the room to question you to the point that we'd fuck like that."

I sighed. "But you let Romeo interrogate me first."

"I needed a moment, Chloe. Seeing you again threw me off balance."

I know exactly what you mean.

"I won't apologize for what we just did."

Me neither. "I... I wanted it too, Franco."

"But that wasn't why I came into the room."

"It just happened," I finished for him, owning up to my part of the spontaneity of it all.

"I trust that Romeo got all the answers that he could out of you, anyway." He looked at me seriously, as though he was trying to grapple with this situation of seeing each other in the last way either of us could ever have imagined.

"Will I be a hostage here?" I asked.

He studied me again, that brooding and solemn expression so stark on his face as he shut the water off. Keeping me waiting for a reply, he focused on grabbing towels and continuing to be attentive. While he didn't dry me off, he took his time wrapping me in the towel and looking me over, as though he needed to constantly reassure himself that I was here, in the flesh, and not his imagination.

"Franco? Will you and Romeo keep me here?" I didn't want to ask for how long. If he thought to secure me here for good, that would be kidnapping. While I knew he was in the Mafia and the Constellas weren't above performing that crime, I needed to know why they would need me any further.

"Now that I've answered your questions…"

He grunted. "You're that anxious to run away again?"

I swallowed and broke eye contact, intimidated to admit that yes, I was. His affiliation with the Constella Family was always a main point of contention between us. My parents never approved of Franco back when we dated, and they'd be pissed to know that we'd reconnected despite the circumstances. I'd struggled against the prejudice of Franco being in the Mafia for so long. I knew that his actions toward me could never be something *he* considered as himself, but as a dutiful member of the Mafia.

"Look at it this way, Chloe," he said as he walked back into the room to get dressed. He pointed at the clean clothes someone had dropped off, gesturing for me to use them if I wanted to instead of putting on the clothes he'd taken off me in a hurry. They lay scattered on the floor. While they were mine and I didn't want to be indebted to Franco or the Constellas, I refused to put them back on. They were too stark of a reminder of the bloodbath I'd narrowly escaped.

"You're in the witness protection program."

"*Your* version of it," I clarified.

"Something like that." He finished dressing and crossed his arms as he looked me over. Still clad in a towel, I felt underdressed and vulnerable. As though that one quick fuck was not nearly enough to scratch the surface of how much I'd missed him.

"Because you witnessed a crime committed against the Constella Family—"

I gaped at him. "Manny and Suzie were just the managers of the neighborhood deli!"

"Which is in a building owned by the Constellas."

I rolled my eyes. "So you take anything as a turf war?"

"A building," he continued despite my snark, "where we hosted different operations in the basement level."

I cringed. "What… kind of operations?" I felt sick, worried that they tortured people down there or deposited bodies… I slapped my hand over my mouth and gasped.

"What?" He frowned. "Do you remember something else? You shouldn't have ever been allowed down there as a new-hire deli worker."

"Please tell me that dead people weren't stored in any of the walk-in freezers or fridges."

He rolled his eyes. "No. The basement was used for packaging."

I narrowed my eyes and waited for more.

"Of products. Like drugs. Not bodies."

I exhaled in relief. "I… I was never in the basement."

"As you shouldn't have been. Manny wouldn't have slipped up. He was well aware that the deli was a cover business."

Slumping to sit on the edge of the bed, I felt weary of these details. I was so sick of struggling with life, and now I had to come to terms that my new job that was supposed to have been a restart on life was just a cover-up for a drug packaging operation.

"A crime happened on Constella property. We can't determine why, nor can we determine who could have done it."

I tensed, trying to look like his words didn't impact me. But they did. He might not have a clue, but I had my suspicions. Remaining quiet, I stared at him and willed him to say his piece and go.

"What?" He stared at me, noticing that I clammed up. Try as I might, I couldn't fool him. He was too damn observant, especially, I figured, where I was concerned. Back when we were in love, he'd made it his mission to memorize every inch of me, inside and out. He knew my body, but he had a damn good idea of how my mind worked too.

"Nothing."

"Why'd you hesitate?"

I sighed. "I'm just sitting here."

"And anxious to run away again."

Maybe… not. If the person who had the deli shot up was who I thought of, perhaps I'd be smart to stay where Franco could protect me for once.

No. That's stupid. I shook my head, both in an attempt to clear my wishful thoughts and to dissuade him from the ready-made assumption that I was hellbent on fleeing.

As if I could even escape this guarded house.

"I want to help you, Chloe. I'm sorry that you were caught in that shooting."

I gazed at the sincerity in his green eyes, blazing with a firm sense of sadness that lingered. He should hate me. He could loathe me, but I knew he meant it when he didn't wish me ill.

"But I can't help you if I don't know everything."

God, no. I was *not* prepared to come clean, not about the one thing that would ensure he'd hate, loathe, and scorn me.

"Did you tell us everything?" he demanded, full of authority but not being malicious.

I nodded, swallowing down the taste of the unspoken lie so bitter on my tongue.

No, Franco. Not even close.

9

FRANCO

Knocks sounded on the door, pulling me from staring at Chloe. I wished it could be so simple, that looking at her like this, expectant and letting her see the disbelief and suspicion in my expression, would tempt her to come clean and tell the truth. She used to do this same silent-question look with me, too, urging me to spill whatever I didn't want to share with her. That was how well we used to read each other. How well we used to effortlessly operate on the same frequency.

Because something warned me that she wasn't being honest. Not completely. The catch was that she'd gotten better at hiding herself.

I sighed and opened the door, letting Danicia in.

"Hi," she said to Chloe before addressing me. "How are you feeling?"

Battered. Mixed up. Confused. But she wasn't talking to me. I thought that letting Romeo question Chloe would be the breather I needed to handle being in her presence again. It wasn't. After losing my control and sleeping with her, I needed more than a breather. I needed my head set back on right again.

"Fine." Chloe raised her brows, suspicious of the tall woman who entered.

"This is Danicia," I introduced belatedly. "She formerly headed up an ER department, but now she works for the family."

"Ah." Chloe clamped her lips shut.

"And I heard that you got knocked out," Danicia said, not reacting to Chloe's mild snark.

"It's just a mild headache…" Chloe said.

"Humor me," Danicia said. "I'll take a quick look and make sure there's nothing to worry about."

"I'll be back," I told the women. I doubted that they'd need privacy to make sure there wasn't a concern about a potential concussion or anything, but it would be better if I stepped out.

As soon as I strode down the hall, I wondered what she could be hiding. Chole and I hadn't seen each other for ten years, and a lot could happen within that time. From what she did share, some things didn't add up.

Like why she moved so often.

Or why she wanted a job that paid under the table.

And how she managed to stay on the move without caving to her parents' pressure to stay where they could control her.

I sighed, running into Andy and Vic, two guards who'd served the family for many years.

"Franco, we got a situation."

I rubbed my face. "We *always* have a situation." I didn't mean to gripe, but right now, in the aftermath of seeing Chloe again and fucking her, I didn't want to focus on work. I wanted to focus on *her*. On any remnant of *us*. I gave my life to Dante and the family, and I seldom ever allowed myself to be greedy and put myself first.

I knew what I was getting into when I signed up to serve the family, but today, I wanted a break.

"Sorry, sir," Vic said.

I waved him off. "What is it now?" I hadn't stopped concentrating on the A&J Deli shooting yet. This was the way of the Mafia life, though. "Situations" came when they did and often overlapped. Life was never dull around here.

"The Giovannis are trying to get into the gambling rooms at the Hound and Tea building again," Andy said.

"Goddammit." Dante and Romeo cleared those assholes out of there not long ago, but it seemed that the lesson hadn't sunk in.

For the rest of the night, I assisted the men at the gambling rooms. It was late by the time I got back to the house Chloe was staying in, but that didn't stop me from stopping in her room and checking on her.

She was asleep, lying in the bed with her limbs out. A small smile teased at my lips. She was never still in her rest, always moving and flopping around as the most restless sleeper ever.

I didn't bother her, wanting her to be rested, but come morning, nothing would hold me back from questioning her and probing for whatever she was hiding. Because she was. I knew it.

The next day, though, she wasn't available. She wasn't in her room, and the housekeeper explained. "Miss Eva came by and asked Miss Chloe if she'd like to have breakfast in the big house."

"Thanks." I yawned as I left. I slept like shit last night. I couldn't blame my late night of supervising the latest "situation". I could fault Chloe for keeping me tossing and turning, though.

At the house Dante shared with Nina, I found Chloe nestled in with the other women. Nina, Tess, and Eva all chatted with Chloe. It seemed like a women's sort of gathering, so with a quick glance at Chloe, I grabbed some coffee and a pastry to find the boss.

I didn't get far. Danicia crossed paths with me and acknowledged me with a lift of her chin. "Franco. Good morning."

I bit into the pastry. "Uh-huh. Morning." I wasn't ready to consider it a good one yet. I was tired, and I had no further information or hunches on what Chloe could be hiding from me. Her return in my life was sudden and conflicted, but I was too uninformed and that was never a good feeling.

"She seems fine," Danicia said, knowing without my asking what I'd want to hear. "Nothing to worry about physically."

"Good." I stepped forward but stopped again. "What do you mean?" Why'd she emphasize *physically*?

"Well, she's so guarded, I can't say for certain the trauma of what she went through isn't making an impact on her."

I frowned, hating that she'd suffered through it at all. Chloe was too good, too sweet to have the difficulty of a violent life. I knew that back when we dated, too. It was the hardest part of trying to convince her to give me a real chance.

"Please let me know how else I can help," she said before we parted ways.

I would. There was nothing I wouldn't do for Chloe. Even if I despised how she'd broken my heart, I could never want her to suffer. Seeing her slightly less frosty with the women in the kitchen warmed my soul, but after hearing what Danicia said, I wondered if she was just covering up her problems.

She was covering something up, and I wanted to know what.

I reached Dante's office and found Liam sitting there. Romeo as well. It looked like they'd brought their breakfast in here. Liam extended his leg to shove out another chair for me to take.

"We found her purse at the deli," Liam said.

"Oh, yeah?" I raised my brows. "Anything of interest?"

"That depends on what you're looking for," Liam said.

I glanced at Dante, feeling the weight of his stare. He would've remembered who Chloe was to me. All those years ago, I went directly to the boss himself for reassurances that Chloe could move in with me. He promised, of course, that my significant other would be protected the same as the rest of the Constella Mafia women were. It hadn't made an impact on persuading Chloe to stay with me, though.

"I'm looking for the identity of who shot up that deli," I replied, as I was expected to. If Dante was waiting to hear me say that I wanted to pursue leads on Chloe, he'd be waiting until his death. I didn't need to vocalize that I wanted her again. It should've been implied.

"Do you think Chloe is involved with the shooting?" Liam asked.

I shrugged. She was hiding something from me, and until I knew what, I couldn't be certain in my answers. I wouldn't let anyone torture the truth out of her, and no one would try, knowing who she was to me.

"Her purse had cash, a ChapStick, two mechanical pencils, and a dying phone."

I raised my brows at Liam. "No ID? No cards?"

He shook his head. "Nope."

"That's it?" I asked. That didn't sound right. "What'd you find on the phone?"

"Nothing."

I deadpanned at him, then glanced at Romeo and Dante. They didn't react, clearly having heard this odd detail already before I entered. "Nothing?"

"No call log. No contact lists. It's a very limited model of a smart phone, and there is no browser history, apps, pictures, anything. There is nothing on that device."

I shook my head. "How?" Frowning, I followed up with, "Why?"

"Seems like it's a burner, or she's using it as one." Romeo shrugged. "Maybe she's on the run?"

"What, from her parents?" I scoffed. Judge and Mrs. Dawson were pompous pricks. They'd see to her staying on the right side of law and never having to hide a criminal history. That right there was why they were so against my dating her, against us loving each other in our youths. I was that "bad Mafia boy" who could never be good enough for her.

"I can see why you two didn't hook up. Or stay together." Liam whistled.

I huffed a dry laugh before I sipped my coffee. "You look her up?"

He nodded. "Yeah. I figured it was fair game, seeing as she's the witness in this case of the shooting." Furrowing his brow, he got more serious as he watched me. "And after I saw how numb you went yesterday when you saw her, I thought it would be wise to be as informed as possible. In case you are too close to her and all of this to remain impartial to what's happening."

"Franco can and will stay diligent," Dante answered, speaking for me. He was right, but I felt a tug of guilt too. I'd never had to choose between Chloe and serving the family. I found a way to have the best of both worlds by asking her to stay with me as I began my career for the Constella name. *She* was the one who ultimately chose not to be with me.

I couldn't help but glower at Liam. I wasn't mad that he looked into her. I expected that sort of due diligence from him, the same as Dante knew he could count on it from me. I didn't care for his implication, though, that a large enough obstacle stood in the way between Chloe having a future with me.

"We loved each other, though," I told him, not shy about speaking the truth. "Or so I thought." She couldn't have cared that much when she opted to run from me. "And that love should've been stronger than her parents trying to control her life."

No one argued me there, and I was grateful when Romeo changed the subject, sort of. "We gave her the purse at breakfast, but perhaps we can trace her calls if she uses it."

And hides using it. Why else would she go so far as to cover her calls and have damn near what amounted to a burner?

I was due more answers, and I resolved to ask her again for the total truth after I finished my coffee. I nodded at him. "If she's hiding something, we'll figure out what it is."

"Agreed," Liam said. "I'm hoping to ride along with you to the warehouse, though."

I furrowed my brow. "Why? What did I miss?"

"A few more Giovannis were fucking with another business," Dante said. "Stefan's getting really desperate, thinking he can mess with us all over the goddamn city like this."

"But you still don't think Stefan's behind that shooting at the A&J?" Liam asked.

I shook my head. "I think something else is up." But I chugged the rest of my coffee and set the cup down near the other empty ones near where Dante's kitchen staff would come by and pick them up. "Come on. Let's go check out whoever's at the warehouse."

Because after, I had a date to get answers out of Chloe. It wasn't until hours later that I had a chance to do so. Liam ended up sticking with another soldier while I returned to the house where Chloe was being guarded.

I couldn't shake the suspicion that she might have an idea who shot up the deli she'd just started working at. Without any way to track much of her recent history, it seemed more and more likely that she could know what happened. Our hackers had no info. She was lying low, it seemed. Working jobs under the table. Not using credit cards.

Who are you hiding from?

I had yet to dismiss how she'd clammed up earlier. As I walked down the hall toward her room, I slowed in my steps, catching the sound of her voice through the door.

"I miss you too."

I stopped. Going still, I held my breath and wondered if I heard her correctly.

You miss who? The affection was clear in her voice, and I hated the instant flare of jealousy that streaked through me. *Who the fuck is she talking to?*

"I don't know, Caleb."

Caleb? Did I hear that right? It sounded like she said *Caleb*, but maybe it was something else, distorted with the muffled sound traveling through the closed door.

Did she say Caleb? Is she talking to another man in there? No guard would've let anyone inside, and I knew she had to be using her phone that was returned.

My heart broke again. Whatever solid piece of it that remained shattered with her speaking to a *man* with such a loving, caring tone.

I didn't wait. I turned the doorknob and entered, catching her in the act of swiftly lowering the phone from her ear and hanging up.

10

CHLOE

"**A**m I interrupting something?"

I blinked once and tried to breathe through the panic. The sensation of terror was an old friend. Fear constantly hit me, and I wondered how my heart could take it anymore.

I was safe here. Guards wouldn't let anyone in. I wouldn't be harmed, even though this was a Mafia location. But I was *not* safe from him. Franco presented a live and real threat with him glowering at me like that, so serious and cautious.

If he'd come a moment earlier...

If he'd popped in a second ago...

Swallowing hard, I strained to convince myself that he didn't know. I had to believe that he was unaware that I had a son.

The moment Romeo and Liam went to breakfast and gave me my phone, I was desperate to use it and call Caleb. He was fine. I was certain he was having the time of his life in Brooklyn with his friend. Ethan was a good, solid man who'd keep his grandson, Brent, and Caleb safe.

After all the danger and fright, after being on the run, and definitely after the way Franco and I reconnected yesterday, I had to hear my son's voice. I needed the confirmation that he was all right while I worried I never would be.

"No." I cleared my throat and tried to say it again, stronger. "No. You're not interrupting."

He wasn't in the mood to buy it. If he hadn't popped in so quickly, so suddenly, I could've had a chance to prepare myself. I was stuck between too many emotions to keep a mask on. Heartache at not seeing my son cut through me. I wanted to keep talking to him and hear his little voice. Sadness at knowing I was failing as a mother weighed me down. I wished I could provide a better homelife for him. But most of all, I was seized with anxiety about what Franco would do if he found out about Caleb.

He can't know. Not like this. Not now. Not ever. He would never, ever forgive me, and knowing that felt like such a cruel letdown from how good it felt to be with him yesterday.

"Who were you talking to?"

"Just checking on something," I said. Trying to look and act braver and stronger than I felt as I hid my past, I furrowed my brow and attempted an expression of being offended. "I did have a life before you brought me here."

"Who is he?" he asked, not budging from whatever impressions he'd made. I didn't know how much he'd overheard before he walked in through the door. Thinking back, I realized that I didn't say much to my son. Mostly, I listened to him going on and on about a dinosaur program at the museum that Ethan took them to that morning.

I stared back at him, waiting for an answer to come to me. He must have heard enough to hear Caleb's name. But there was a chance that he hadn't, and I didn't want to give away anything. This might be nothing more than him assuming I had to be talking to another man, some stroke of jealousy.

"Do you have a man on the side?"

"On the side?" I snapped. "We had sex yesterday, Franco. It's not like I've been sleeping around with you for a pattern or a…" I growled, frustrated with how quickly he could insinuate that I was up to no good. All I wanted to do was survive, to get by and do the best I could for my son, dammit.

"Do you have a man who's going to be looking for you?" he repeated.

The first time he asked it, it sounded like a question born of envy, of jealousy, as though he hated the idea of me with anyone else. As if he had any right to that. The second time he asked if I had someone else who'd notice my absence, it came across as more of a security detail. That he'd need to be aware of someone coming after me while I was here under their version of witness protection.

"No." I shook my head, annoyed but still worried. "No, of course not." Forcing myself to lift my head and look him in the eye, I added, "I wouldn't..." I heaved out a sigh. "I wouldn't have had sex with you if I wasn't single."

He closed the door behind him, seeming to need a moment to let my replies sink in. I had no doubt he was cross-checking what I said with whatever prejudices and assumptions he wanted to cling to. When he settled back to face me, watching me with that unbreakable stoicism, I couldn't read him.

My ability to guess what he was thinking must have gone rusty over the last ten years. I had no clue whether he'd push, or why. Clearly, he'd want to know if I was contacting someone who'd pose a threat to the Constella Family. But was that it? Was that all he wanted to know? If I was a threat or complication he couldn't allow in his life?

"Are you sure about that?" he asked.

"Am I sure that I'm single?" I huffed out an incredulous laugh. That follow-up question hit too close to the truth. His obvious doubt about my relationship status was eerily spot on.

"You have a burner phone with no contacts. No ID. No credit cards. Your purse held nothing of significance that could be tracked. I'm not out of line to guess that you're hiding something, Chloe."

My heart raced again. I felt the tension in my back as my shoulders slumped. It was instinct to curl forward, to want to protect myself from any incoming danger. He stood still, menacing with his hard glare, but he didn't make a move to advance at me and wound me.

"Tell me the truth." He furrowed his brow, as though the suspense of this conversation ate away at him. "I can't help if I don't know the truth."

You can't know it all. There was simply no way I could tell him about Caleb. Not now, not after so long.

"There…" I drew in a deep breath. *Do it. Tell him. Just fucking get it off your chest.* "There might be someone who doesn't think I'm single."

His expression remained hard and guarded, but he exhaled in such a way that suggested he'd been tense and holding his breath. "Go on." Again, the command in his tone was unmistakable but not mean.

"My ex is a very determined man."

He looked to the side of the room, narrowing his eyes with anger. I couldn't tell if he was mad to hear that I had been with someone else or that I had an ex who wouldn't give up on me. It had been ten years. Franco had moved on, too. He had to have. A man as strong and sexy as him couldn't be celibate for a decade. And it was weird for him to assume I could've been stuck on him, on the past, and not attempt moving on as well.

"Keep talking."

"My ex is a…" I rubbed my hands up and down my thighs, nervous to even mention Wes. He belonged in a carefully locked up compartment in my mind, in my past. But we weren't. Not with his constant presence as he pursued me.

"He's a prominent man whom my parents adore."

He grunted a dark laugh. "Did they set you up with him?"

I shook my head, but I shrugged on the tail end of that gesture. "I don't think so, but it's possible. I met him after I'd left town, but they're in the same circles."

"When?"

"When what?"

"When did you meet him? When did you leave him?"

He wasn't cruel or harsh with his demands for answers, but the act of talking about my never-ending nightmare dragged me down into the pit of hopelessness I had to pull myself out of—again. Closing my eyes and lowering my face into my hands, I took a moment to gather my wits and calm down enough to talk. I couldn't explain a thing if I was crying.

When did I meet him? I wished I'd never met Wes. I rued the day we crossed paths at all.

When did I leave him? He made it sound like that effort was a one-time thing.

Tears stung behind my closed lids. Stuck in the darkness of my memories, I was transported to each and every time I tried to get away from Wes.

"Chloe." His voice was softer and closer. I barely registered the sounds of his footsteps as he crossed the room. Only when his warm body pressed against my side did I realize that he sat next to me on the edge of the bed. His thigh pushed against mine and his arm wrapped around my back. Feeling his power, his muscled form holding me closer, I fought through the need to bawl.

He was right here, pulling me back to the present, and I wanted to cling to the security he offered.

"Talk to me. Please."

I sniffled, lifting my face. Resolved to get this out, I nodded and wiped away the few tears that slipped out.

"I met him seven years ago. He came into the diner I was waitressing at while I tried to finish my courses, and he was interested right away."

"*He* was interested while you weren't?"

Caleb was only a baby then. I didn't have time to date. "I wasn't available to date anyone. Not him, not anyone, but he was persistent. We were only together the first time for several months, not even a year, but after I left him and moved, he found me again and tried to get back into my life. Rinse and repeat."

"When you say seven years ago..." He narrowed his eyes. "Does that mean he's been doing this all that time?"

I nodded, hating how weak I sounded to admit that I'd been running for that long. "He's very possessive. And abusive. He only slapped me around a couple of times, but he's mentally manipulative, a master of emotional abuse."

The muscles in his arm tightened around me as he pulled me more against him. This much closer, I felt the racing tempo of his heart beating so wildly in his chest. He was enraged at this news, but I wasn't victorious in that realization. If Franco was mad or riled up, violence would follow. That was who he was, but I didn't want to recognize that gritty, darker side of him.

"You've been on the run for years from this asshole?" he asked.

I nodded. *And you. Running from the truth of our past that I'm still scared to share with you.* "More or less."

"When's the last time you saw him?"

"I..." I exhaled a long breath. "I've gotten better at hiding so he can't follow me, but he still does. He's got resources I can't beat."

"When, Chloe?"

"Six months ago," I replied. "He found me in Philly, and I moved here to get another new start. But it's the same dance and song. Every time I relocate, I swear he's right there behind me, stalking me because I dared to leave him."

He rested his hand on my thigh, rubbing slightly. "You mentioned him slapping you around." The words left his mouth with difficulty, as though he gritted his teeth to say such a thing. His anger was a palpable force that hung in the air, but I noticed how carefully he tried to rein it in.

"Yes. He prefers mental abuse. Narcissism on steroids."

"Has he ever escalated to hurting you in any other way?"

I shook my head but I zoned out, staring at his hand on my thigh. As I stiffened from his question, he stopped rubbing my leg. I missed the soothing caress and tensed when he lifted his hand to put two fingers under my chin. He tipped my head up so I'd look him in the eye.

"Has he ever threatened to hurt you in any other way?"

I swallowed hard, forcing my throat to work past the emotions clogged there. I nodded. "He's... he's..."

My lower lip trembled as I struggled to get the words out. Franco dropped his gaze there. His brow furrowed deeper, etching lines of concern on his rugged face. In his green eyes, I saw the pain he suffered through *for* me. The idea of this man being so empathetic, this trained killer, to soften and feel so much for me... It was enough to start attacking the walls I'd built up around myself.

"He's threatened to kill me." *And Caleb.* That was my biggest fear, that he'd make good on that threat.

"Fuck." He pushed out a harsh exhale as he slid his hand over to cup my face. "Chloe... Fuck."

"When you say you can't determine who shot up the deli, I worry that it could be him." I cleared my throat, determined to get through this and speak up now that he got me to open up at all. "I worried that it wasn't an attack on your men or your business, but an attack on *me*. Just like he's always promised."

He firmed his lips into a thin line, but I was on a roll.

"I'm sorry. I'm sorry that I didn't tell you yesterday. I've been keeping under the radar and trying to handle him as much as I can without anyone else suffering, but..."

"No. That ends now, Chloe." He stared into my eyes as though he wanted to will me to believe him. To believe in him and what he said, but I already had a crappy track record with that. I didn't believe in *us* all those years ago, and now look where I was.

"I'll look into him. I will keep you safe. No one can hurt you here."

My heart swelled with relief. I wasn't stupid. I knew that his saying that meant something serious. The Mafia didn't mess around with threats. As much as it bothered me to think of someone being murdered, I appreciated that he could want to step up and see to my security regardless of how I'd broken his heart and left him so long ago.

"Thank you."

He tilted my head closer to press a chaste kiss on my forehead. "For seven fucking years... He's been after you all this time?"

I nodded. "I wish I could go back in time and redo what happened in the past."

"All of it?" He raised his brows, seeming defensive now. "Even me?"

Lifting my hand to rest it on his chest, I got lost in his troubled gaze. He sucked me in. He pulled me closer and drew me to care more and more.

"Meeting you?" I shook my head. "I can't imagine not having you in my life, the way we were back then."

His jaw slid. "Do you wish you could go back and redo the time that you left me?"

No. He couldn't understand why I did.

I shook my head, not as an answer of no, but a show of how this conversation broke me down. "I will never regret you, Franco. Never."

11

FRANCO

Even though Chloe was emotional and seemed to be on the verge of breaking down, I noticed the difference.

She said she never regretted *me*. But she couldn't say that she didn't regret *leaving* me the way she had.

"I can't ever regret you, Franco." She licked her lips as she lifted her watery gaze to mine. Her hand came up to slide along my jaw, and I couldn't help but lean into her touch. I'd missed it. I'd longed for her tender sweetness for so many years, and I was beholden to her affection again.

Staring down into her blue gaze, I saw every bit of the open vulnerability shining there. She was trusting, but still so scared. She was opening up, yet holding back.

Too much time had passed between us for this conversation to go differently. Yet, I refused to let her think she couldn't rely on me. I had to convince her that I was here for her and that no matter the distance between us, I would protect her. She had my heart. She always did. And that wouldn't ever change.

The delicate stroke of her soft fingertip on my skin rocked through me. Such a gentle caress, and it coursed through me so fiercely. Any connection with her would hit me hard, but I refused to tumble back onto the bed and take her hard again. I couldn't fuck her senseless as a diversion from what needed to be shared now.

Truths. She had to come clean, fully honest about anything and everything she wanted to hide from me yesterday.

Stroking her hair back from her face, I kept her snug against my side. But I was firm in the decision that I wouldn't take her again. Not hard, nor gentle. I couldn't let sex dictate all that came between us now.

"You don't regret me, yet you can stand by your decision to leave me."

She lowered her gaze. Shame and pain filled her face, but I tipped her head so she'd look me in the eyes again.

"Chloe, I need to know why you ran. Why you ran from me."

She sucked on her lower lip for a moment, hesitant. "It was ten years ago."

"It wouldn't make a difference if it was ten days ago. Why, Chloe? Why'd you run from me if you loved me?"

She tried again to look away, but I deserved more. I was due the truth. I lifted her chin again. "Why couldn't you fight for us, for us to stay together?"

"You don't understand," she replied on a shaky whisper. Tears leaked from her eyes, and as they streaked over her cheeks, I wiped them clear from her soft skin. Even though she couldn't see me, she didn't make a move to shy away or cower from my direct gaze.

Watching her crumble and break apart was hard. It broke my heart to witness her suffering and crying so softly like this, like the sadness and despair had to slip out because she couldn't bottle it in and hold it captive any longer. If I was the key to unlock the dam of all that she'd kept in, so be it. If she needed me to firmly ask for long overdue answers, then I would persist and beg for her to explain.

I had to know. I was due an explanation. I would hold her and let her soak my shirt with her tears. Determined to have an answer after all this time, I would wait for her to overcome her emotions and reach a point where she could explain.

Tears were a weakness—from my enemies. Deep, heart-felt sorrow was a grievance—from anyone who dared to come against the family.

Chloe was the exception. She would always be my exception. My life was full of danger and threats, of violence and death. Darkness had to rule sometimes, and I embraced how skilled I was at dealing it out, of being the family's top capo.

I didn't give mercy to anyone. No one.

Except her.

This beautiful soul was the *only* exception in my life, and she always would be. It was the biggest reason I used to think we made so much sense together. That we were so compatible as extreme opposites. She was soft and sweet and delicate to express tender emotions while I had to train to be hard and mean and wield my power with ill intentions. She was the light to my darkness. The Yin to my Yang. It united us. Our love and acceptance of each other tied us closely together in that deep affection, but still, it wasn't enough to keep us as one.

I never saw her as weak and prone to wishing for peace. She never held it against me when I had to be cruel and harsh. We were opposites, but stronger together.

"Help me understand," I said as I rubbed her back. Giving her a moment to collect herself, I waited in suspense for her to speak.

"My parents wouldn't approve of us," she replied.

This again. I shook my head slightly. "They didn't approve of our hooking up in the first place. They told you not to date me at all, and you didn't listen."

Her shoulders slumped as she sighed. "I know. I couldn't have stayed away from you then."

"But you could stay away for ten years?"

"I couldn't see a way forward," she replied. Her tone was firmer, bolstered with more surety and confidence, but I couldn't tell if she was sticking to that line because she believed it or because she'd rehearsed it so many times that it sank in.

"I couldn't see a way forward to be with you and to avoid the wrath of my parents."

"Fuck them, Chloe." I grunted, confused how they'd have so much control over her. "Fuck them."

She rubbed below her eyes, still getting over the tears. "It's not that simple."

"Then simplify it for me," I said. "What am I not understanding? You said you loved me—"

"I did. I wasn't making that up."

"And you know how much I loved you." I was careful not to say it in the present tense, that I loved her currently as well. That was too big of a power for her to know she held over me. That I was still as crazy for her as I was back then.

"It would have been so damn simple." I tucked her long, golden locks back and ducked to her eye level. "You could've lived with me. Dante had already approved it. You could have moved in with me while I trained and started my career. You would've been protected."

She sucked on her lip, showing me her tell for when she was debating what she thought and wondered.

"I know that we're different people, that I'm supposed to be this big, bad wolf your parents never approved of. But you know me, Chloe. You know exactly who I am. I can't change who I am, where I come from, and who I work for. But you would've been safe with me. You would've been protected and cared for. Safer with me than under the influence of this ex who's stalking you."

She furrowed her brow, staring at me so solemnly. "I wish I could've been protected. Wes is a horrible asshole. He was terrible to me."

I gritted my teeth, keeping as tight of a leash as I could to rein in my anger. Fury coursed through my veins, heating me up with a rage I couldn't wait to vent. I would, but not on her. I couldn't right now. Not until I knew why our love wasn't good enough to fight for.

"He was manipulative. Abusive. And every time I tried to leave him, he'd find me."

"How?" I intended to find out every fucking detail about this guy so we could take care of him for her. I'd be asking her for information about him. Right now, I wanted to focus on getting an explanation for why she left me. That was the priority in my mind. It was the main mystery I needed an answer for. Still, I couldn't help but ask about this fucker she could've been spared ever meeting if she'd stayed with me.

"Every time I left, my parents would tell him where I was. It took me a while to wizen up and get some street smarts about how to lie low."

"And it never once occurred to you to seek me out?"

"Years had passed, Franco." She frowned at me. "You can't blame me for thinking you would be so mad and hurt that I left in the first place."

I was angry and so wounded. "But you still could have relied on me, Chloe. Always. When I gave you my heart, I did so knowing you'd have it forever."

She wasn't convinced. I saw the doubt in her eyes. She'd been on the run and trying to hide from this guy for so long, fear and anxiety ruled her well.

"It's not that simple," she argued softly. "He would've only tracked me here. I suspect he has, and he shot up my workplace to prove that I'll never be safe from him no matter where I go."

"I dare him to come find you here." I reveled in the confidence shining in her eyes. Just sitting here and talking gave her strength she hadn't realized she could find in me. "He won't get past me."

"How can you care?" she asked, curious in an almost sad, dejected tone. "After all I did to dismiss our love, how can you be so quick to come to my defense?"

"I always will, Chloe. You can count on that."

She looked at my lips. When she met my gaze again, I saw the lust building in the bright blue brilliance mesmerizing me to never glance away.

"You can count on me for anything you need."

She twisted toward me, lifting her other hand to slide up my chest until she draped her arm over my shoulder. "Even another chance to forget it all? For just another moment." As she pressed her lips to my cheek, I closed my eyes at the delicate, sensual offering she presented me.

"How?" I asked, knowing damn well what she meant.

"Make me forget. Make me forget all the years we've spent apart," she said, leaving soft, barely-there kisses along my jaw.

"That's what I need, Franco. I need you. I want you to show me that all that matters between us is what we share right now."

I growled slightly, frustrated with keeping myself in check.

"I need *you*," she repeated, a breath away from a kiss as she leaned into me. I caught her arms, both to keep her steady from falling over me and pushing us both back onto the bed and to maintain distance.

As I held her at arm's length, she was temptation personified.

I needed her too, but I still wanted my damn answers.

She was *still* hiding something, and until I was sure that she wouldn't spring any more surprises on me, I had to keep my wits about me.

Easier said than done with her.

Especially when she closed the inches between us and crushed her lips to mine.

12

CHLOE

I couldn't resist kissing him. I didn't want to hold myself back from sealing my lips to Franco's.

He grunted at the force of my lunge at him. At the first touch of his soft, firm lips so warm against mine, he gripped my arms tighter. His fingers dug into my skin, and I reveled in the bite of pain.

I couldn't bear his staying back. Even though I saw the hesitancy in his eyes, I hated the idea of us being parted when we were both right here. Together. Finally, after all those years I was only able to dream and fantasize about him, missing him from the bottom of my heart, we were together, in this room, and opening up.

While I had yet to share *all* of the truth with him, I felt better about telling him that Wes wouldn't let himself be a person in my past. It was freeing to unshoulder the burden of my ex stalking me, and I relished the lightness of not being stuck under the pressure of that worry that Wes could've arranged for the shooting at the A&J. I'd mourn Manny and Suzie, but I was relieved that I'd opened up to tell Franco about my suspicions, that Wes might be the man they're looking for.

He opened up, too, pleading with me for an explanation of why I ran. It had to take guts and a lot of submission to ask me for an answer I couldn't give him.

But that give and take ended there.

I couldn't tell him that truth—not yet. I couldn't reveal the fact that I had a son, that he was involved in the creation of my family.

All I could do was show how badly he would always be the one for me. Taking the initiative to go for him, to lean into his body heat, I wanted to show him what I struggled to put into words.

I needed him. Despite all the years we weren't together, I had to make him understand that I loved him and needed him with all my heart. Even though he stuck to his assumption that I hadn't fought for us back then, my love was his and my soul would always be tied to his.

"Chloe," he growled as he moved his hands. He didn't hold me back. Now, as I dove back for another, deeper kiss, he hauled me closer.

I dreamed of his gritty voice full of desire. So many nights, I'd envisioned this very moment and this exact heated kiss.

"Fuck, Chloe. You—" His protest, if that was what he wanted to get out, was lost as *he* kissed *me* harder.

I fantasized about this heady sensation of being under the command of his mouth on mine, his lips parted, meshed so hot and wet against mine, and we both explored again. I tasted him and knew my soul was whole again. He sucked on my tongue, pulling me closer and drawing me deeper into this intoxicating spell of desire.

In my darkest moments, this fiery love was what kept me strong. And during my loneliest trials of missing what we had together, the hopes for his hands so strong and firm, keeping me close, were what pushed me to endure it all.

"You—"

"I need you," I repeated, firm in wanting to reconnect with him.

I had to show him how much I meant it, and I started that by crawling all the way onto his lap. I pushed his head back, slamming my lips to his, but he didn't fall. He didn't rock backward on the bed. Scooting his butt back, he made room for both of us, him seated and me straddling his lap. All the while, he framed my face and kissed me back.

As soon as my knees landed on the mattress, I sank into the plush bounce and found my balance—as one. We were flush together. His hard chest was a wall of power to brace my softer curves against.

I wasn't as lean and thin as he might remember, but when he lowered his hands to grip at my sides, I got the impression that he enjoyed this too. He curled his fingers, clutching me as though he'd never want to let go again.

Kissing him as though air could no longer matter, I ground against him. From the rub of my aching breasts, feeling so heavy with my arousal, and the downward grind of my pussy over his erection trapped under his pants, I covered him with all of my body.

Blood rushed through me, pulsing faster as I fell into this heady thrill of desire. My heart hammered, and as I kissed lower down his jaw, angling for his neck, I felt the rapid beat of his, racing just as fast as mine.

His hands roved everywhere. Every way he moved, it was another effort to keep me close. He pulled on the small of my back to ensure I rubbed down over him, slowly humping him despite the clothes between us. He grabbed my ass, forcing me to spread my legs wider over him. And he gripped my head, cupping the back of it to plaster his mouth to mine in a harder, hungry kiss.

"I need you," I repeated as I tugged his shirt up.

He lifted his arms, and the only break we gave ourselves in kissing each other was to let that layer come off.

His chest heaved with hard breaths, and I took a moment to run my hands over the dips and valleys of all the muscles. He'd always been so strong and obsessed with fitness. Over the years, he'd earned a chiseled body decorated with scars and tattoos.

"I need *all* of you," I begged as I grabbed the hem of my shirt and tugged up.

"Fuck, Chloe." He moaned into my mouth, making out with me as I reached back to free my breasts from the confines of my bra.

"So gorgeous," he praised as he stroked his hands over my sides.

Once he took my breasts in his hands, I raised up on my knees higher. Offering myself to him, I wordlessly prayed that he'd taste me there. I arched my back, thrusting my nipples toward his wet lips, and he didn't disappoint. He braced his big, callused hands on my back, keeping me right where he could reach me and torture me some more. With hot kisses, long licks, and hard sucks, he tormented my nipples. He was ravenous to sample every inch of me, and as he held me up, I tried to undulate against him and seek friction for the aching neediness I felt for him. Only him.

Back then and now, Franco drove me wild.

"I…"

God, I couldn't speak, breathless and weak to this desire lancing through me. I wanted him so damn bad. I wanted his dick deep inside me and reminding me how we belonged together. I had no right to him. I had zero right to ask him to give himself to me.

He was already hurt that I'd left him the way I had—without a goodbye and no chance of a reason.

If I were to tell him that I had his son, that I gave birth to Caleb without giving him a hint that he would be a father, he'd be hurt even more. I'd wound him. I'd break his heart all over again. The fury I'd instigate would never fade, and for that reason, to spare him more pain, heartache, and anger, I had to swallow down the words. It was on the tip of my tongue. I was bursting to tell him that I needed him to listen to me, that I needed him to know that he was the father of my son.

But right now, I needed to *feel* him, to reconnect and build on the love that I was so brave to give up so long before.

It never died. The love between us would always burn so stubbornly bright, but I had no power to change the fact that obstacles would always remain between us.

Tell him. You have to tell him. The urgency to come completely clean raged within me, but I feared that he could find out too soon and be mad. I worried that he'd never forgive me, and in that manner, I decided to be selfish, to be greedy for once, to put myself first and go for what *I* wanted, what *I* needed.

I had the chance to be with him now, right here, and I wasn't strong enough to pass up on it.

I eased back, crawling away from him but still leaning forward to kiss him. Aiming for the edge of the bed so I could stand, I ended up on all fours, crawling away. My breasts swayed with the motion as I retreated. When he leaned in, chasing after me and kissing me, he lifted his hands to cup my breasts and rub his thumbs over my nipples. I moaned, feeling every touch shooting straight to my pussy. A live wire of tingling desire threaded through me, but I resisted the urge to fall onto him. Not yet.

Standing shakily, I hurried to remove my pants and panties. He wasn't far behind me, pushing his hips up to take off the rest of his clothes too.

I took a moment to look him over, admiring the stiff hardness that jutted up from his lap. He was so thick and long, and I knew exactly what kind of pleasure and pain stretching myself on him would give me.

I set one hand on his shoulder as I crawled back onto the bed, but with my free hand, I wrapped my fingers around his dick and stroked the length of his erection.

"Chloe." He gritted his teeth as he urged me back to him. "I won't last."

"Me neither," I whispered before straddling him again. Kissing him hard and slow, I angled his cock to my soaking wet pussy. The first push of his wide head on my entrance filled me with so much pleasure that I wanted to be greedy. I wanted to take all that I wanted from him. The only thing I could count on in this moment was an orgasm, a heady, all-consuming release. His love would become conditional the moment he learned about our son and how I'd lied to him.

At this moment, though, I wanted what he could give me.

I sank down his rigid dick, treasuring the wide, stretching fullness. He speared up into me at my pace, and I did my best not to hold my breath or tense up. It burned as he entered me fully, but it was such an exquisite sense of being pushed to my limits that I knew the reward of taking all of him would be bliss.

"Chloe," he growled again, his voice so thick with need and longing. I heard the agony of all the heartache, and I vowed to try to erase as much as I could. It would always linger. Our past would be etched into the fabric of our lives, but right now, I had the power to show him that I still cared, that I still needed and wanted him.

"I missed you," I breathed against his parted lips. Up and down, I rode him. Starting slow guaranteed us a lead in to the friction we both chased. Once I sped up, making sure to drop down to the point where I rubbed my clit over him too, we were on a race to come.

"I missed you every fucking moment you were gone," he said, his ravenous stare locked on my tits as I bounced on his dick.

I leaned back, giving him the show he wanted. If he wanted to watch my breasts jiggle and bounce, I would arch my back and let him look his fill. If he wanted to thrust up into my pussy, I'd widen my legs that much more to welcome him in as I sank down.

The angle left me unbalanced, but he didn't let me suffer. Holding my back, he gave me support, and with this leverage, I used all my strength to slide up and down his cock until he came.

I beat him to it by seconds. As my pussy clenched and waves of pleasure soared through me, he roared a guttural sound of relief. I moved, rocking on him until I wrung out every last bit of ecstasy between us. I came with the intensity of floating, of drifting, of coming apart into so many pieces that I wasn't sure how I'd feel whole again.

He flooded me with his hot cum, jerking deep inside me—where he belonged.

Shaking and breathing hard from the rush of reaching my orgasm like that with him, I nearly slumped onto the floor. But, of course, he didn't let me.

"Come here," he urged gently. His voice was gruff from coming, but he was tender as he wrapped his arms around me and hugged me close.

I'd wanted to come to him so many times over the years, but until I could tell him what held me back, I felt like a fraud, a selfish, horrible person to want what I could never have.

His love, forever and unconditionally.

13

FRANCO

"So, you first met your ex in Santa Fe?" Romeo asked Chloe. She nodded, pulling her lower lip between her teeth as she seemed to concentrate. "I want to say it was mid-April. Yeah. Mid-April. I was almost through my spring courses when we met."

That was specific, and I appreciated how concise she was trying to be. Yesterday, when she admitted that an abusive ex had been stalking her, I wanted to burn the world down and hunt him until he cried for mercy. Chloe was too sweet, too innocent to ever warrant or deserve some asshole targeting her and wanting to hurt her.

Wes Morrison was his name, and he would pay for his sins. She told me a little more about him last night when we both suffered the same dose of insomnia, waking up in the middle of the night. Today, though, she was determined to shed her fear and shame and tell Romeo, Liam, and one of our best hackers more information so we could track him down.

"He came into Benny's, the diner I was waitressing at, and started talking with me." She glanced at me. "It was a diner near a strip club, and that wasn't an uncommon occurrence with the late hours of the diner being open. Men would walk from the strip club and still be in that, uh, mentality of seeking women. All of us waitresses would be hit on." She shrugged. "He didn't stand out at first, and he was really charming. That was his 'thing', to lay on the charm so thick that later, when he changed to being an asshole, you were duped. Like it was hard to believe that this super slick and sweet man could possibly be such a jerk."

I shook my head, hating every second of her reliving this. She remained calm, though, with her hands folded on her lap in the big living room.

"I *hate* men like that," Eva said as she sat and handed Chloe a glass of water.

My distant cousin, Dante's niece, wasn't always involved in these matters. She was a part of the organization, though, the princess of the Constella Family, and she wasn't ever out of the loop. Liam suggested that she sit in on this chat in case Chloe would want the presence of a female.

"I think it's fair to say anyone would hate any man or woman like that," Romeo added.

"After a couple of casual dates, I could tell that Wes was interested in a lot more. He was really lovey-dovey, really trying hard to impress me, and given how..." She sighed. "Given how lonely I was, I was likely an easy target. He bent over backward to impress me and be sweet to me." She looked at me, struggling for a moment. "I was very lonely."

Her words hit me hard. *Why? Why did you ever make yourself feel that way? I was here, available for you.*

"I was working nonstop. When I wasn't working, I was taking my classes. I left Beckson with a scholarship, but it only went so far. I still had to pay for expenses, and I refused to ask my parents for any money." She licked her lips. "I went out of my way to go no-contact with them."

I narrowed my eyes, trying to understand. "You left town and never spoke with them?"

She nodded, lowering her gaze.

Then why didn't you come with me? If she left her controlling parents, why not come to *me*, come start a new life with me? I would've paid for her classes. I would've given her everything she wanted. The main reason that she split from me was because of her parents' disapproval. If she burned her bridges with them anyway, why not do it to be with me in the end? This news stung an already open wound.

"They didn't like that, though, which is why they sent Wes to find me."

"Like a PI?" Romeo asked.

"No." She sighed. "Wes was a cop who'd stayed in the force long enough until he went into politics. He doesn't hold an office, but he's affiliated with many influential people."

At the word *cop*, we all shared a glance.

"Oh, boy." Liam raised his brows.

Romeo smirked as the hacker typed away, faster.

"Wes came from money, and that's how he knew my parents. I'm guessing my father knew him through his job, as a judge, and they formed an acquaintance of some kind. They wanted to know what I was doing, and eventually, Wes came clean about how he knew them and tried to persuade me to come home and visit." She scowled, shaking her head. "When I found out that he'd come all that way, stayed months trying to get in my pants, I was pissed. I dumped him on the spot, but he was persistent, trying to break me down."

"Why did your parents want you to come home so badly?" Liam asked.

"They're very controlling," Chloe and I said in unison.

"Anyway," she said, "I refused. Each time he tried to come back into my life, I would shy away from him, not give him the time of the day, and plan to move again. And again. For a while, I think he just wanted to do as expected. Maybe they were paying him to retrieve me or something. After a while, I think it evolved into a game, some sort of sick, twisted ploy, like an obsession. That's where I learned to leave as little of a trail as possible. No cards, watch my internet use. All of it. I've been trying to start over with nothing traceable."

"He's no longer a cop, though?" Liam asked.

"No. But I think he has enough connections that he can find out whatever he wants," she replied sadly. "I was very careful coming to New York. I got a decent job through a friend in Philly, but when someone shared a video that went viral and I was walking by in the background, he found me."

"Damn. That's shitty luck," Eva said with a wince.

"Yes. But not as shitty as thinking I could be anonymous here, one among so many in the city, then having my new workplace shot up." She rubbed her face. "If the deli was shot up because of Wes, it's my fault Manny and Suzie are dead."

I rubbed her back, wanting to console her. "Has he ever used force or shot at you or anyone in your life before?"

Romeo frowned at me. "I'm not sure Wes shot up the A&J himself."

I nodded. "He'd hire it out, but still." I looked at Chloe expectantly.

"No." She shook her head. "I know he's got a gun. And he's trained with firearms from his time in the police department he started at before he went into politics, but he's never escalated to that level of violence. He's always stayed on the down-low. The most he'd ever done to me physically was slap me around a few times, mostly just backhanding my face, but that was it."

That was it? I fumed at that phrase. Like this fucker raising his hand to her wasn't so bad in the scheme of things. Sure, a backhand to the face was nothing compared to being shot. However, neither of those were okay—at all.

If Wes was responsible for the attack on the deli, that was a significant change in his intentions. If he wanted to stalk her and just follow her, then that was one thing. Engaging in a shooting like that—even hiring it out to be done on his say so—that was an entirely different matter.

So, why would he change it up now? Why try to shoot up her workplace now, after seven years? Even though Chloe's suspicion had some substance, I couldn't be sure that the shooting at the deli was because of her being there and her stalker ex wanting to see her wounded or dead. The attack happened on Constella property—a place where drugs were packaged and distributed. It could have been a hit on the Family.

"Did you give away anything that could've had him tracking you here? Use anything that could be registered anywhere?" the hacker asked. "Cards, phones, anything?"

She shook her head. "No. I learned from my mistakes, unfortunately. From trial and error, I figured out what he could use to find me, and I avoided those things."

Liam followed up with more questions, and Romeo did as well. It was a thorough and extensive investigation, and Chloe cooperated through it all.

"I think that's all for now," the hacker said. He stood, tucking his laptop under his arm. "I'll take this back to the office and have my team do a deep dive." With one more nod at us, he took his leave.

"If I think of anything else, I'll let you know," Chloe said, rubbing her eyes. She was still so tired, and I couldn't blame her. Fucking each other like we did last night would wear a person out. Plus, it had to be mentally taxing to relive the experiences she'd suffered under Wes's abuse and stalking.

"Want to hang out by the pool for a while and unwind?" Eva asked as she stood, smiling at her. "I'm pretty sure the others would be up for a swim or soak."

Chloe raised her brows. "Now? In this weather?" She glanced at the window. While it was still chilly, some signs of springtime showed outside.

"No, no. The indoor pool." Eva tipped her head in the direction of where that enormous conservatory-like room was.

Chloe opened her mouth wide, giving a silent *Oh, wow*.

Her parents were wealthy, but it sounded like since she forsook them and left, she had been living penny to penny. All to get away from her ex. An ex she never would have met if she'd chosen a life with me, like she promised she would.

Enough. Stop. It wasn't so easy to tell myself enough was enough, but I wasn't sure what to think anymore. I'd spent so long hanging on to this bitterness that she left me, and now that she was present and we'd reconnected to some degree, I wasn't sure how to act around her.

"Am I… allowed?" she asked, looking up at me. "Can I go with her?"

I nodded. "You don't need to ask permission. You're not a prisoner here."

She arched a brow.

"You need to stay on the premises, under guard, though. Until we know who attacked that deli where you happened to be working, you have to stay safe and hidden."

"Come on. It'll help," Eva said, coaxing Chloe to follow her out of the room. She'd find her a suit or whatever she needed.

I was glad for the break from her too. "Did you look at the report that he found?" I asked Liam and Romeo about what the hacker sent us all just before we met here to talk with Chloe. I skimmed it, but I'd reread it later.

"Yeah. Wes Morrison is connected to the law firm that Elliot Hines worked at," Romeo said. He narrowed his eyes as he mentioned that attorney's name. Tessa, his fiancée, was expected to marry the creepy man. Romeo killed him, though, not only because he wanted him out of the way so he could have Tessa for himself but also because Elliot Hines represented Reaper, the Prez of the Devil's Brothers MC.

"That's what I noticed too," I said. Ever since—no, before—Dante met Nina and pretended to date her, we'd been facing off with the Devil's Brothers MC and the Giovanni Family. It seemed that every which way we looked, there was another connection to one or both of those groups. And now it looked like Chloe's ex was tied to our enemies as well.

"We don't need more damn people after us," Romeo said.

As Nina neared the end of her pregnancy, we were all on edge. Dante was protective of her already, but with a baby here, he'd be really cautious.

"Then let's take him out," I suggested. "Let's find Wes and remove him from this situation. If he shot up A&J's to scare or hurt Chloe, he'll pay for it. If he ordered that deli to be attacked to hurt us, as a message from the MC or Stefan, then he'll pay for it."

Liam and Romeo nodded, glancing at each other and in approval of that plan.

I shrugged. "It'll be one more thing removed." Personally, it'd be my honor to kill the man who'd dared to hurt the woman I loved.

"We'll plan it. I'm sure the tech guys will track him soon," Liam said.

I held up my hand. "And Chloe won't need to know. All right?" I looked them both in the eye, silently conveying that this would remain *our* plan, among us.

She already thought I was a ruthless, evil killer, and I didn't need to taint any image she had of me. If we could ever try to forge ahead in a new future, I didn't want her to have more reasons to cast me as the bad guy she shouldn't be with.

14

CHLOE

Eva led me to the vast, high-ceilinged room where a pool and hot tub awaited. It was situated back here in the mansion that several of the Constellas seemed to call home.

I was stunned. Rooted in place at the door to the greenhouse-like space, I dropped my jaw and stared.

I grew up on the "right" side of the tracks in Beckson. It was small-town life, but with my father as a judge and my mother as a PhD-holding former professor, I was born into wealth and privilege—both of which my parents lorded over me and everyone else they came in contact with. From a young age, I was expected to know there were two kinds of people in the world, the haves and the have-nots, and only select individuals could be worthy of my time.

Meeting Franco in junior high showed me how wrong they were.

Seeing this place that Dante Constella owned demonstrated how the supposedly inferior caste of people my parents looked down upon were *really* loaded.

"Damn." I blinked and tried to let it sink in that this wasn't a dream. I was here, in this mirage of luxury. It felt like a fever dream. After witnessing the bloodbath at the deli, being on the run, and fearing for my life from those shooters, it seemed surreal to be here with nothing more than the expectation to unwind.

Eva laughed lightly. "It's impressive, huh?"

"More than." I huffed a weak laugh.

"You haven't met Olivia yet," Eva said, smiling at an adorable blonde toddler.

"I…" I smiled at the little girl. She was so cute in her teeny bathing suit, tugging a lady by the hand to reach the pool sooner. "Oh. She's precious." I hadn't grown out of the baby fever stage yet. Caleb had just turned nine, so old now, and I missed the baby days. Trying as they were, I savored them.

"This is Liam's daughter—"

Nina waddled up, interrupting Eva. "Your daughter. Eva. You're just waiting on the adoption papers to be finalized, but that's just a technicality."

"Mama!" Olivia said as she held her arms up so Eva could pick her up.

"Sounds like she thinks you're her mama," I said, smiling at the cute child as Eva picked her up.

"Swim, Mama. Swim!" Olivia pointed at the pool, and we all laughed.

"She's a tyrant," Tessa said as she joined us. "Practically a dolphin already."

Eva gestured for me to follow her and Olivia into the shallow section. "As soon as Liam came here with Olivia, Dante suggested having her swim back here. It was already cooler before the holidays, so I think it's safe to say that she's made this *her* pool room."

I shivered in delight at the warm water. "Ooh. It's heated."

Nina held on to the rail as she eased in, aiming for a chair in the shallow end. This was no ordinary pool, but a custom made one. "Yes. Heated enough to mimic a hot tub but not so hot that I can't enjoy it." She grinned, leaning down onto the chaise.

"Dante insisted on starting Olivia with swim lessons as early as possible," Nina said. "But I don't think any of us could have realized how quickly she'd be obsessed with it."

I saw how she loved the water, swimming out independently without Eva holding her, but within reach. Caleb would have loved to have a place like this to swim when he was younger, but I only could take him to public pools when they were open and I had time off work.

Seeing Olivia reminded me so much of Caleb, and my heart panged with sadness. I missed him. He was the light of my life, but in the context of the last few days, I was so damn grateful that he was away on spring break.

But if I am stuck here after the end of his break... I wasn't sure what I could do. If I asked Franco about how I could leave this so-called witness protection program, I'd need to explain why. And telling Franco about the son I never shared with him...

I cringed slightly, not liking this chain of thoughts.

"He can't wait to be a daddy again," Nina said, rubbing her stomach.

She looked ready to pop. "How far along are you?"

"Thirty-six weeks."

"Almost there," I said, smiling. Being with these women and Olivia wasn't something I would've imagined with the ideas and preconceptions I had of what the Mafia lifestyle was like. My parents spent so many years trying to brainwash me into thinking that Franco and his family were thugs. Gangsters. Lowlife criminals who only wanted to take drugs, party, and kill.

This family scene before me was cozy. Surrounded by wealth, yes, but these women weren't awful. Nina and Tessa were engaged and happily settled. Eva had adopted this adorable little girl who seemed so happy and carefree. They weren't oppressed and forced to be slaves or servants to their men. They weren't stuck in bedrooms as concubines and told what to do.

They were just... members of a family, hanging out and splashing around.

"Chloe?" Eva said as she swam closer to me and sat on the ledge under the surface. Tessa played with Olivia on the other edge of the pool. "Can I ask you something?"

I nodded. I was guarded, but she had been nice enough so far.

"Did you run from the deli and not call the cops because you worried it could've been Wes who ordered the attack?"

I sighed and nodded. "Yes. I didn't think to grab my purse when I ran out of there. I just wanted to escape and live. But even when I stopped at that motel, it didn't cross my mind to call for help. Because it could lead him to me."

The other women swam up close. Olivia floated on a kiddie raft as she poured cups of water into a funnel toy with spinners.

"Hey, no gossiping without us," Tessa said.

"We're not gossiping," Eva said and rolled her eyes. She glanced at me. "No secrets among us. I told them what you said about your a-hole of an ex." She covered her mouth to whisper the almost-bad word.

"I figured as much."

"That we'd talk?" Nina said.

"You all do seem very close," I commented. Oddly, I wasn't mad that they knew about my situation.

"If we're not close already, we will be once we start getting married. Nina will be my stepmother-in-law," Tessa said, which earned a laugh out of Nina. "And Eva will be my cousin-in-law."

I raised my brows. "That's a layered connection. How'd that happen?"

One by one, they shared how they'd come into the Constella Family. Nina was rescued by Dante when she was lost in a bet to a biker leader. Tessa was also saved by Romeo when she was raped. And Liam entered the family, bringing Olivia with him, when he joined as a soldier and fell in love with Eva.

All their stories punched out more bricks in the wall that I was supposed to keep up in assuming this Mafia family was all bad. Deep down, I knew the Constellas couldn't be criminals. I always knew that Franco was in the family, and it hadn't stopped me from falling in love with him. Had I not gotten pregnant when I was supposed to come to New York with Franco, I would have toughed through the garbage my parents told me and come to be a Constella Mafia wife ten years ago.

Now I saw what I was missing out on. The Constellas were a Mafia Family, but still a *family*. Dante, Romeo, and Liam hadn't hesitated to protect their relatives and their women. That didn't make them evil. It made them heroes.

"I can't believe you knew Franco when he was younger," Tessa joked. "I imagine he was just as much of an exercise-junkie hard-ass then as he is now."

I smiled. "He was always working out," I said.

Eva and Tessa asked me a few more questions about *how* I knew Franco back when we were younger, but I didn't have to suffer the pressure to speak much for long. Olivia, bless her sweet, little heart, saved me. She started to fuss because it was time for a snack. One of the house staff came by, and the lure of her offer for apples and crackers beat staying in the pool.

"I'll come grab her in a few minutes," Eva said. "Thank you."

Fortunately, no one asked about my past with Franco again. I bet they were really eager for the gossip, but the slight shake of Eva's head told the other two not to bring it up.

Thank you, Eva. Thank you. She was aware of our past, or at least whatever Franco told her about why I left. She seemed to get it that my history with Franco was a complicated and messy topic that I wasn't ready to get into at the moment. She said coming to this room and swimming would be a chance to unwind, and she was sticking to that offer.

"I am so nervous that I'll have to have a C-section," Nina griped as she settled back on the chair. "Every appointment I have, they say that my pelvis is tilted." She winced as she got situated, clearly at the stage of nothing feeling comfortable.

"But if you have a C-section, won't that prevent you from stretching out your hoochie and being loose?" Tessa teased.

Nina splashed at her. "Argh. I don't want to hear about that, either."

"It's not so bad. It all goes back to normal." The second the words left my mouth, I froze. I locked my body in place and didn't exhale, tense and freaking out that I blurted that. Of all things to toss out casually, that shouldn't have been it.

They took notice, looking at me with raised brows.

"What?" Tessa asked.

"You have a child?" Eva asked.

Shit. Shit. Shit. I had to backtrack out of this. They couldn't know that I had a son—the son I never told Franco about. I worried enough that he'd never forgive me for hiding that from him, no matter how justified I thought I was in my choices regarding that secrecy. With these women giving me such a warm and easy welcome into their little group, I couldn't risk their hating me and not forgiving me for my past as well.

I cleared my throat. "I… gave birth," I said. It wasn't a lie. "But the baby didn't make it."

Technically, both of those statements weren't lies.

I had a miscarriage when I was dating someone in college, but no one needed to know about that. It was the first time I had sex after leaving home, after having Caleb. I hadn't cared about the man, but I wanted to see if I was able to move on from the memories of Franco plaguing me, if I could be intimate with someone else. Newsflash—I didn't. The sex meant nothing, I didn't even come, the condom broke, and I lost that baby. It was enough to turn me off from wanting to date. It also confirmed the impossibility of casual sex helping at all. It was just before I met Wes, and once he entered my life, I had zero chances of wanting to find a man again.

"Oh, my God." Tessa set her hand on my shoulder. "I'm so sorry."

"That's terrible, Chloe," Nina said, frowning. "I'm sorry for your loss."

None of them pushed to know if it was Franco's baby, but I grew more nervous under Eva's careful stare. She nodded, pressing her lips together in sorrow. "I'm sorry to hear that," she said sincerely, but I felt like she had to be wondering and thinking.

If she got it in her head that I was talking about Franco's baby that I lost, she was wrong. I supposed the miscarriage counted as a baby I lost, and I had given birth—to Caleb. Even though I meshed the two truths together, it still worked as a lie.

The baby in the miscarriage hadn't been carried long enough to be considered a viable pregnancy to begin with. I was still so young, and it just didn't work out. While the event saddened me when it happened, I figured it was fate's way of letting me know it wasn't meant to be. So many women suffer miscarriages all the time, and when I learned I was one more number, a statistic among many, I moved past it.

I could *not* tell these women the truth.

I did know a thing or two about childbirth because I had a child. I had Franco's son. Caleb was the reason I joined the conversation and tossed out that the whole stretching fear was more of a myth. That was my experience I referenced, not the early-stage miscarriage with the one-night stand in college.

But they couldn't know the whole story. They couldn't have this raw truth. I refused to let them learn my deepest secret before I could tell Franco.

As I lowered my gaze to the water, I drew in a deep breath.

I had to tell him. We'd had sex twice now, and while I still had no direction of guessing what could happen next, I couldn't let this guilt grow and increase pressure on me when I was selfish to want him so intimately. It wasn't fair to either of us to carry on like this with my huge secret looming large between us.

I had to let Franco know my hard truth, and then, only then, would I be able to accept that we could truly start over with a clean slate of complete honesty between us.

If he'd even want me after I tell him that I hid his son from him.

15

FRANCO

The hackers found information on Wes. He didn't try to hide anything about himself, and there was ample information about him to collect. Before long, we had many options of looking into Chloe's ex, but it would take time to wade through it all and see what was important for the sake of removing him as a threat to Chloe and for any potential involvement he could've used to coordinate an attack on the Constella Family.

That was how we ruled—with no mercy for those who didn't deserve it.

Wes was previously a cop in two different small towns before he left and went to law school. Then he hopped around, apparently not worrying about his income since he came from generational wealth. With that long-standing wealth came powerful influence, and he shaped his career into that of a politician. While he didn't officially run for any positions or roles, it looked like he was preparing to campaign one day.

What Romeo and I focused on was how to find him *now*. Fortunately for us, he had an office in the city where he was supposed to meet with an up-and-coming entrepreneur from Canada. Unfortunately for him, we'd make sure he was dead and missed that meeting.

There wasn't a single chance of his getting away with what he'd done, and I wasn't in the mood to wait for the hackers to compile more details. The man deserved to die for ever raising his hand to her and causing her to live a life on the run, always hiding.

But Wes was not there.

A couple of soldiers came with us, and while Romeo and I waited for the men to capture him and take him right out of his office and bring him down to us, we stalled and watched the time pass in the alley.

"He's not there," Vic said. He leaned over to speak through the window. "Doesn't look like he's been there all day."

"Dammit." I pounded my fist on the steering wheel.

"Maybe we were too hasty to think we'd find him on the first try," Romeo told me. "We only just started looking into this. I'm not saying the hackers screwed up, but maybe this fucker has had practice at covering up his whereabouts."

I nodded, frustrated, but I agreed. I couldn't let my impatience for justice get the better of me. This wasn't only about Chloe. We had to also see through the shooting at the deli.

"Did the staff say anything?" Romeo asked.

"No," Vic replied. "None of them said shit."

The other soldier shrugged. "Want us to go back up there and force answers out of them?"

I shook my head.

"I left a couple of bugs in there. We can record what's said," Vic added.

"Good," Romeo said, dismissing them.

I drove away from the area, annoyed but taking it in stride. This was only day one of looking into him. Not every hunt went quickly. These things could take time.

"The two men you and Liam shot at the motel showed up in the database," Romeo said after reading through something that came in on his phone.

I glanced over, seeing that he was skimming through a text.

"The hackers got back with me. It looks like the two men who shot up the deli were just hired killers. No affiliation with any group, but one of them was previously wanted as an accomplice for murder in Tennessee."

"But no connection to Wes?" I asked. "Or the Devil's Brothers? Or Stefan?"

He shook his head. "No. Just a mention that he could've been a former soldier for the Domino Family."

I huffed and shook my head. Sometimes, it seemed like we were pulled in so many different directions. Life would never be peaceful, but for fuck's sake, it was too damn difficult to identify who shot up that deli now.

"As soon as we get a lead on Wes, we'll go after him. We'll look for him again because we won't give up on this." Romeo put his phone away, turning to glance at me. "We'll get answers from him before we kill him."

"Definitely," I agreed.

"And with those answers," he added, "you'll know who is to blame for that attack."

I furrowed my brow, not following why he'd state the obvious like that.

"And then you won't need to keep Chloe under our protective custody."

I heaved out a sigh. I didn't want to think about that. "I'm not letting her out of our protective services until her ex is gone."

"That's valid. But after Wes is gone, will you be able to let go of her?"

I clenched my teeth, hating how good he was at putting me on the spot like that.

"You haven't let go of her all those years you weren't together."

"I know." I checked my mirrors again, seeing that the soldiers still drove behind us.

"Can you let her go again?"

"I—" Slamming on the brakes halted me from finishing what I wanted to say. It also prevented me from slamming into the car that sped out from the perpendicular alleyway. It shot out in front of us, blocking me.

"What the fuck?" Romeo slammed his hand to the dashboard. We both reached for our guns as the soldiers driving behind us screeched to a sharp stop as well.

The car that pulled out in front of us zoomed away, and once it cleared the alley, the rumbling roars of engines came closer.

Bikers. They sped up in pairs on their motorcycles. From a distance, their skull logos were noticeable on their leather cuts.

"You've got to be fucking kidding me." Romeo shook his head.

Our soldiers filed out, rushing up to deal with the Devil's Brothers members blocking our way.

"This is getting really fucking old," I muttered. We stayed in the car, letting the soldiers handle the situation. If we stepped out, it might complicate things. Both of us were prime targets that our enemies would love to take out. With the blacked-out windows, though, they couldn't see who was in this car. Romeo and I had a front-row seat to the men threatening the Constella soldiers.

"Very old," Romeo agreed wryly.

"Who is that?" I asked and gestured to the older man near Reaper. If things went south, we'd step out and assist the soldiers, but they were trained for these sorts of things. I had faith they'd get them to leave. This area of the city wasn't as rundown and lawless as the locale where the bikers thought they ruled. If they wanted to start shooting here, the NYPD would be alerted. Civilians in the surrounding businesses would be informed.

"Gunner," Romeo said. "From what Andy has found out, Gunner is Reaper's VP, and he's been itching for an excuse to overthrow Reaper from power."

I rolled my eyes at the gangly older man who coughed so hard I bet his bones were rattling. He looked as mean as a snake, his eyes slitted and his face scowling as he argued with Reaper.

They shouted about whose idea it was to come down this alley in this direction. It sounded like a petty squabble over minor details.

Reaper reminded Gunner that he had no say in this, and that comment made Gunner shout louder yet.

I didn't miss the threat they issued.

"If you drive one more fucking inch this way," Reaper roared, "I'll kill you all."

Romeo and I shared a glance. We faced threats every damn day, but it was becoming an annoying habit for these bikers to think they had any power to tell us how it would be.

"Seems like these clubs have a lot of turnover." I tipped my chin at Gunner telling the other four bikers to retreat. Reaper noticed and he yelled over his VP to order the other four MC men to stay right where they were. Soon enough, they ceased trying to act big and tough with us. They were too involved in their power struggle.

"Someone else will take over sooner or later," Romeo agreed as Reaper and Gunner fought to the point that they seemed to race each other down the alleyway.

"They'll suffer from so much infighting or seeking a new leader," I said as I backed up with the soldiers in their car again and retreated for a different route out of this alleyway. "Then they won't even be a concern for us."

Romeo nodded. "I imagine a new leader might not want to side with Stefan Giovanni, either."

"Not my problem," I said. "Until they make it mine."

"Exactly." After letting out a long sigh, he faced me fully. "You didn't answer me about what I said."

"About Chloe?" I asked, still checking my mirrors for any other surprises or ill-executed ambushes.

"Yes. Can you let her go after Wes is dead, after the A&J's case is closed?"

I shook my head, deciding to be honest. "I'm not sure I can let her go. Not again. I want to keep her for good, Romeo. You know that she's always been it for me."

"I recall," he said.

"I want her forever. We're reconnecting and getting into a little more give and take of information, but…"

He pounced on my hesitation. "But what?"

"I can't shake this suspicion that she's hiding something from me."

And until I knew what that was, I refused to completely lower my guard with her and wind up in a horrible position of *wishing* she were the one for me.

She might need me. She might desire me and miss me. I could also swear left and right that she had feelings for me.

But she couldn't be the one if she lied and hid things from me, right?

16

CHLOE

I slipped underwater, both to avoid continuing this conversation and to cool off. The humidity was so cranked up in this room that I felt overly warm. Or maybe the discomfort of feeling so hot was internal, due to the *oh, shit* sensation I tried to hide.

Once I surfaced, I realized that the women weren't satisfied. All three of them looked at me, and I felt horrible to have changed the mood so drastically. In other circumstances, it could've felt more like I was hanging around on an ordinary afternoon. Now, it seemed like I'd crashed the party.

"I'm... I'm sorry I mentioned it," I said, looking at Nina. She seemed the most troubled about the news and I felt like an ass. The last thing any pregnant woman wants to hear is about the loss of a baby, even one that hadn't developed past a couple of days since conception, according to what my gynecologist told me then. No matter the timing or age or any other details, miscarriages and child loss were serious causes of pain.

Eva frowned, looking off to the side. She was clearly uncomfortable, but Tessa stayed by my side and looked ready to offer me support.

"It's hard to be a statistic like that," I told Nina. "But it's true. So many women suffer from miscarriages and..." *Okay, I don't think I'm helping.*

Nina nodded and rubbed her big belly. "I was so, so nervous in the beginning of the pregnancy," she admitted.

"Did you suffer any difficulties in the first trimester?" I asked.

"Just the usual. Some morning sickness. Fatigue. Danicia and my Ob-Gyn kept telling me that my pregnancy was coming along as expected. No worries. No concerns."

"But it's hard to accept that and *know* there's nothing to worry about," I commiserated.

"Yeah." She furrowed her brow. "And now that I'm getting closer to the end, I'm obsessing more about the fear of the actual process of childbirth and all that."

"I think every woman on the planet feels like that the first time," I said. I caught myself from saying anything about how scared I was. They were under the impression that I didn't have a child. They were in the dark about Caleb. I couldn't offer personal advice or general suggestions and platitudes about childbirth if they didn't know I had a child. "Every woman probably feels like that *any* time they're getting ready to have a baby."

Tessa nodded and smiled. "Yeah. So this one can be a practice round," she joked with Nina. "Then when Dante knocks you up again, you'll know what to expect the next time."

Nina laughed dryly. "No. I don't think I'll be in a rush."

Tessa rolled her eyes. "Yeah, right."

My nervousness faded the more that the focus shifted to Nina, but Eva brought it all right back to me. "Chloe?"

I faced her, anxious about how closely she looked at me. It felt as though she was searching for a clue on my face.

"This baby you lost. Was it Franco's?"

I consciously forced myself not to freeze or flinch at her direct question. They were all watching me so seriously that they'd be able to pick up on any tell I might show.

"No." I swallowed hard, hating myself. Again, it wasn't a lie. The baby I lost in the early-stage miscarriage wasn't Franco's. But it felt like such a crappy coverup to the fact that I did have Franco's baby.

"I met a guy in college and the condom broke and..." I shrugged as though to show how little it affected me. It did, but it didn't. I already had Caleb, and the fight that I had to endure to keep him alive and with me was such a horrendous one that the miscarriage for an *oops* of a baby with a stranger hadn't caused too much distress.

"When I went to the doctor's office after the miscarriage, I debated very strongly about having my tubes tied." As a single mother, I wanted no chances of another pregnancy any time soon. "They refused to tie my tubes because I was only twenty—too young, according to their policies."

"Does Franco know about this?" Eva asked.

Shit. She was too damn good and chasing for answers. Eva was observant and quick thinking, so close to being on the right track.

"No." I shook my head. "It happened after he and I... after we broke up." More like after I broke up with him, but they didn't need to know those things to the finer points. "I never thought I'd run into Franco again, especially not like this, and it hasn't come up."

The idea of talking to Franco about pregnancies made me sweat. If I were to bring that topic up, it'd be to tell him that I had been pregnant and carried his son.

"But this is important," Tessa said. "A miscarriage is a big deal, even if you have accepted it and moved on from it."

Not as big of a deal as hiding his son from him...

"And if you're going to be staying with Franco and..." Nina cleared her throat. "Reuniting..."

I shook my head. "No. That's not... I can't even begin to think of how I'll stay and just hop into his life like this." It was already so hard seeing him the way I did, out of the blue and at the moment I needed him to save me the most, but thinking about staying here for good was a torturous tease.

I didn't know what I was doing with him, sleeping in his bed and having sex. It was natural. We were still crazy for each other and drawn to each other with such a fierce instinct. But...

"I'm only here to be protected until whoever ordered that deli to be shot up is caught." I licked my lips, hating the sound of this fate. "The only reason I'm here is because I witnessed that attack and they want to investigate."

"Well, sure," Nina said. "That's part of it."

"That's all of it. I'm not going to stay here for long." I hated saying such a thing. Now that I'd found Franco again, I felt drawn to keep him forever this time around. If he were to kill Wes this minute, I would still have obstacles in my way. I would still be stuck with the lie of having his son and not telling him about it.

"Do you want to stay with him?" Tessa asked. She raised her hands. "I don't know all the details and all, but even I can see how different he seems."

"Franco is a different man," Eva confirmed. "You meant so much to him when you were both younger and so in love. He has never gotten over you. Even with how your parents tried to tear you apart."

God, if you only know the whole truth about that.

"I'm not sure that you're right when you claim that you can't stay here for long." Eva narrowed her eyes. "Do you want to?"

I swallowed hard. Having a real future with Franco sounded too good to be true. I would love to be included in this family, with these women and enjoying their companionship. I would be thrilled to come clean about being a mother and be here for Nina to give her the support I wished I had in a sister or friend in the childbirth stage. I would be so thrilled to bring Caleb here and know he'd be accepted and safe.

Deep down, though, I struggled to convince myself that I'd ever fit in. No matter how much I might wish for this happily-ever-after I destroyed ten years ago to actually have a successful retake now.

Despite everything that lured me to want to stay for good, to tell Franco that I loved him and I always would, I couldn't shake this nagging little warning that it wouldn't work, that I was too different from this closeknit group. That I was an outsider looking in.

I'd spent too much time being forced to stay on the other side of the fence—on the "good" side, the legal side. I was taught to always keep the Mafia thugs out of my life.

After a lifetime of being discouraged from associating with Franco and the people he called family—all very protective and generous people I wanted to get to know better—I struggled to overcome the sense of going for the forbidden, going for what I wanted and saying to hell with the rest of the world.

If my parents could go so far as to send a man to bring me home once, what would they do if they tried to extricate me from the Constellas now?

Fear for my life—and Caleb's—mounted all over again. I was under the illusion of safety here. I was behind locked doors and kept secure by patrolling guards. Franco would defend me.

But my parents would never give up their hatred of the people they called criminals and thugs.

How far would they go if they learned I was defying them by staying with Franco and the Constellas?

I wasn't sure I could risk their wrath and find out.

17

FRANCO

Romeo and I stayed out after our run-in with the Devil's Brothers. Another call came in about issues with a Giovanni spy lurking around another one of our properties, and we went there to check it out.

After the shooting at the A&J Deli, we had to relocate and shift around some parts of our drug packaging and distribution efforts. With so many properties throughout the city, we had options to count on. It still required patience and planning, and in the process of moving things around, we had to consider the increased security needed in setting up the packaging area.

We met up with Liam and another soldier, and before I realized it, it was late at night by the time we decided to head back to the houses.

Dante texted me earlier, letting me know that the women invited Chloe to stay in a guest room in the big mansion instead of the other accessory house where she was first taken. He wasn't asking for permission to move her. He was the boss, after all. But I appreciated the heads up so that I would know where to find her.

Once I arrived, I checked in on her and saw that she was sleeping well. As tempting as it was to wake her and bring her to the brink of coming with me again, I resisted. She needed her rest. Danicia had a good point—she might suffer for a while longer from the emotional hits of trauma from the shooting at the deli. I imagined she was running ragged from *years* of being on the run from Wes and hiding from her stalker.

I stood there for a long while, wondering if I had all her truths now. She'd been holding back from telling me about her stalker ex, but now that I knew about Wes Morrison, I wanted to assume she wasn't keeping anything else from me.

But I feel like she's still hiding something. I didn't blame her for being guarded around me. Not with the way her parents tried to turn her against me for so long back then. Yet, I couldn't put my finger on why she seemed so cautious around me. She couldn't lie and suggest that she didn't want me. I felt how she did. I saw the love in her eyes. But something else was bothering me.

Who is Caleb?

That was the biggest thing that I kept circling back to. I caught her speaking with someone but I had yet to push on who she could've been speaking to. While I could have the tech guys try to track her call, I wanted to be able to trust her to come clean.

With a sigh, I turned and went back to my room. It was early yet. She'd only been here for such a short time, and I didn't want to pressure her.

If she loved me, she'd come clean. *Right?*

The next day, I was pulled away on security issues again, this time with the bikers messing with the soldiers we had positioned near their property. A couple of the MC men were trying to claim that a Constella member had raped one of their club whores. The whole thing was nonsense, another annoying example of the trouble we faced from them. Liam and I spent most of the day following up and settling the matter.

When we returned again, I was eager to spend time with Chloe and ask her who she had called. Who this Caleb guy could be.

Yet again, I was foiled from having a chance to talk with her. This time, it was a happy occasion, not another security concern that kept me from being with the woman I'd always love.

"Right now?" I asked Dante after he found me and Liam returning. "You're going to marry her *right now*?"

He nodded. "We're going to elope. Here."

Liam raised his brows and glanced at me. "That's, uh, sudden."

"It's also what Nina wants. And what Nina wants, I'll give her." Dante lifted his chin. "I don't care how and when we get married, just that she's my wife. So if she wants to suddenly elope, right now, here, then that's what we're going to do."

"Damn." I blinked wide. "Those pregnancy hormones are wild."

Dante grunted a wry laugh but smiled. "That's a fair assessment."

Dispatched to get ready for the very sudden ceremony, I stopped by Chloe's room and found her getting ready. She'd come here with nothing but the ragged clothes she wore from her shift at the deli, but it looked like Eva and the other women hadn't wasted any time in getting her something to wear.

"Wow."

She stood, catching a glimpse of my reflection in the mirror. "It looks just like—"

"Fucking prom." I laughed as I walked in, careful not to touch her light-blue gown. It was a sleek, form-fitting spring dress, but the colors and cut reminded me of the dress she chose for prom. "Damn, you are beautiful, Chloe. Always were and still are." Standing behind her, I pressed a kiss to her bare shoulder. "Always will be, too."

She laughed lightly, pulling away from me with a teasing smile on her plump lips. "Oh, no. None of that. That was how you started the process of messing up my makeup and getting my prom dress off that night."

I smiled, thinking back to how this felt like déjà vu. I had kissed her shoulder on prom night and showed her how good it could be when I fucked her from behind. We were still in the early days of having sex then, so soon after she'd lost her virginity to me then.

I growled a bit, staring at her hungrily. "As soon as this wedding is over…" I beckoned her to come to me, crooking my finger.

She continued putting her earring in and walked up close.

"As soon as the celebrations are done tonight, we'll have a reenactment of that night," I promised her. With one last, deep kiss, I left her room to get dressed.

An hour later, I sat next to Chloe in the conservatory. With the evening light, it looked ethereal out here. While the air smelled of chlorine from the pool and hot tub in the distance, the tables and chairs set up over by the plants seemed separate. If they were to search for a venue to rent equal to what was here, it'd cost hundreds of thousands of dollars. But this seemed right. It seemed appropriate. Flowers had been arranged, and we were all present. I supposed simple and minimal were what Nina changed her mind to wanting.

Liam and Eva sat together with Olivia on Liam's lap. Tessa and Romeo were seated together on the other side. And I was here with Chloe. A few others took seats, but it really was just the handful of us waiting for the priest to begin.

"How come she wanted to do this tonight?" I whispered to Chloe. She was new here, but she'd been spending time with the women for the last couple of days.

"We got to talking about childbirth and she was worried about what could go wrong," she whispered back.

I furrowed my brow, worried. "Is there a cause for concern?" Her pregnancy had been fine so far. Dante was obsessive about making sure she was healthy and comfortable.

"No. Just the general fear and anxiety of the unknown, I think." She shrugged. "But she started worrying that something could happen to her during the birth, and she wanted the baby to be born in wedlock, to have Dante's name in case anything went wrong. She didn't want the baby not to have a father."

I shook my head, smirking. "Dante would never let his child go without. He's loved this baby since the moment they found out Nina was expecting."

Chloe nodded, looking out for Nina to come to the small altar area where Dante waited. "And he's such a good sport to do what she wants."

"He always will. Same for the baby. I used to wonder if he thought he'd messed up being a single parent to Romeo."

She frowned at me, so serious all of a sudden. "What do you mean?"

"Well, you know that Romeo's mother died shortly after he was born." I cringed. "Oh, shit. I wonder if that's why she's wanting to elope like this. Because Dante's first wife didn't make it long after Romeo was born and Dante was a single father."

Chloe's shoulders slumped. "Oh..."

"Dante had to find his footing with Romeo. He was running the whole Constella empire while figuring out how to be a dad."

"That's... a lot." She cleared her throat. "I mean, I can only imagine."

"Yeah. But Dante is such a natural. He's a good dad and he wouldn't change that for the world. Ever since Liam brough Olivia, he's been like a grandpa to her. And he'll cover it with being over-protective and worrying about Nina, but he can't wait to be a dad again."

I glanced at Chloe and wondered about her sad, almost apprehensive expression.

"I bet it's hard to balance work and family with your kinds of, um, careers."

I rolled my eyes and took her hand. "We do all we can to keep the danger out of our homes. Look at Liam. He was in the military, right? In combat under a large employer. Now he's doing the same, but here. There will always be evil in the world, Chloe. The Constella Family only deals with it in their own way."

"I can see that." She sighed. "With Wes having his connections with the law, I get it. More than anyone else could. He's used his connections and powers in a corrupt way, and I am very familiar with how the 'good' guys can be evil too."

It seemed like such a sign of growth, hearing this from her.

"I'm still surprised about Dante, though." She smiled as Nina entered the room dressed in an off-white dress that emphasized the baby in her belly.

"How so?" I whispered to her. She met him before, back when we were younger. I brought her to a few cookouts and parties and introduced her way back then. This past week, she'd been with the women more than Dante.

"He's such a businessman. Committed to working and being so gruff." She furrowed her brow and seemed distant with a frown. "It's hard to imagine him wanting to be this present family man."

I leaned closer to whisper in her ear. "We all are. We're all softies under the gruff exterior." I winked at her, wishing she could see that. If I were to ever bring a child into the world, it would be with her. She was the only woman I ever saw as the mother of my children, and if we could be so lucky, I'd move heaven and earth to welcome our child.

Later, after the sweet but short ceremony, we shared a simple yet elegant meal and cut the cake.

"We can have a fancier wedding later," Dante told Nina as she sat on his lap and fed cake to him. "If you want." He rested his hand on her stomach.

"Or," Nina teased back, a bright smile on her lips, "I can live vicariously through Eva marrying Liam."

"What does that mean?" Eva asked as she held a sleeping Olivia against her chest. The toddler was too tired from all the excitement and fun of the night.

"You're the spoiled Constella princess and want it all," Tessa joked. "Your wedding will be outrageous, I'm sure."

Liam shrugged and I laughed.

"Hmmm." Eva grinned at Liam. "I might already have it all."

I smiled at her holding Olivia. Eva had really come around in becoming a mother.

But the smile on Liam's face seemed suggestive.

"I think..." Eva drew in a deep breath and looked at all of us. "I think I might be pregnant."

Nina shrieked her delight, so excited.

"We've been trying," Liam said as he brushed Olivia's hair back from her face. "We want to make sure Liv has a brother or sister."

"So maybe we'll elope too," Eva said.

Tessa laughed. "Count me out. I want to wait."

We all joined in the joke, chuckling. Even though tonight was sudden, it was no less special. We had the ceremony, dinner, cake, and a little dancing. It was family, and that was all that mattered.

With all the changes and hints of more shifts to the family, I couldn't stop looking at Chloe seated next to me and wonder if she was one of them, if she was a new change and addition to the Constella Family. To *my* family.

If she could be mine for real, officially one of us.

She smiled at me, noticing that I was watching her, and I sighed. In this setting and with this mood, it was hard not to see her in a different light.

Not as my ex whom I'd missed, but maybe my bride.

Not as the woman I wanted to protect from a stalker, but my partner.

And not as the witness I needed to question further, but as the woman I loved for the rest of my days.

As we sat with the rest of them, late into the night, I couldn't help but wonder how differently my life could've been if we'd married long ago, like we'd wanted to.

Would I be a father already? Would she be a settled wife and fitting in with the other women?

I couldn't go back and make up for lost time, but when we finally left to head up to my room, I wanted to start the rest of my life with her now, in whatever way we could.

18

CHLOE

There was no way I wasn't getting laid tonight.
Love was simply in the air.
I am so getting some.
It seemed odd to have that thought. It was something I'd think if I were in a committed relationship, going "steady" with a boyfriend.

Franco and I weren't dating. We hadn't even tried to label what the hell we were doing—except each other.

I was here as a witness to be protected. I was expected to stay here while I waited for them to hunt down my ex, who might be behind it all. I didn't think that Dante or anyone else in the family would hold it against me that I'd brought trouble to their building that the deli was in. If Wes wanted to escalate how he stalked me, he would've done that anywhere, anyhow.

Tonight, though, there was no doubt about it that I was Franco's "date" to the sudden wedding Dante and Nina got together so quickly, and it was just implied that I would be with Franco. Tessa loaned me a dress, and there was no question that I'd sit at Franco's side.

All night, I felt the loving vibe of the family celebrating and coming together. When Franco talked about Dante being a father, I suffered the guilt of not telling Franco that he was also a father. Then with the talk about Eva expecting, it was just too much.

I felt Franco's attention on me. It felt as though the ideas of marriage and love, parenthood and family were shoved in our faces, and he reacted by looking at me and "wanting it all" with me, like they'd teased Eva.

"Franco?" I said once he led me to his room.

I felt his attention. I had a strong hunch what he was thinking and motivated by after tonight. He had *forever* on his mind, but before he could get carried away with the notion of us being the next couple to marry like that or announce a baby on the way, I had to tell him about Caleb. It gnawed at me, like a living, festering agony. The longer I didn't tell him, the worse I felt.

But I wasn't getting a word in now.

He kissed me, too damn impatient to act on how he wanted me. With the romantic evening, I wasn't surprised. I'd been suffering the same wishful *what if* thoughts as I watched Dante and Nina exchange vows, as Eva and Liam announced they were expecting. I was affected by the mood of the night too, but I was running out of time. Caleb's spring break soon would be over. I *couldn't* stay here like this without telling Franco all the truth.

"Shh," he hushed, his lips wet from mine as he hovered them a breath apart from me.

I closed my eyes as he kissed me again.

After. After tonight. I'll tell him in the morning. If he wanted to show how well we fit together one last time before I took the chance to tell him the truth, fine.

I lifted my arms to hold him close and kiss him back hard. My heart pounded faster, like it always did when he brushed his mouth over mine with that demanding hunger he never ceased to have for me. I panted, gasping for air as we made out and backed farther into the room.

In seconds, I was aroused. Slick wetness stuck between my legs, evidence of my need for him. My pussy throbbed, aching to wrap around his dick that was already so hard as he pushed me to backpedal toward the bed. And every time he clenched his arms around me, my breasts stung with the pain of neediness.

I needed him to touch me everywhere. I wanted to explore and caress him all over. And he was on the same page.

Instead of reenacting how we'd made love the night of Prom, like he teased before the wedding when he saw me in a dress similar to what I wore that night years ago, we fell to the bed. He wasn't going to take me in front of a mirror, but on the mattress. I didn't care how or where, just so long as I was with him and he was deep inside me.

As we untangled ourselves to remove our clothes, kissing with every movement, he shifted me until I was on my back. I shivered as he trailed down my body, spreading wet kisses from my mouth to my neck, then further south to my breasts as he fingered me and smeared my cream over my entrance. And lower yet.

I closed my eyes and held onto his head as he licked and sucked at my pussy.

"Just as delicious as I remember," he mumbled against my cunt.

"Franco…" I whined, not caring how needy I sounded. He loved it when I lost control for him. He relished how wild I would cry out for him.

"Shh," he reminded me.

We weren't in the other house, but here, in the big mansion where others could hear us.

I moaned, rocking up against his mouth, seeking that release he teased me with. Between his fingers in my entrance and his tongue circling my clit, I was right there. My orgasm was so close.

But I couldn't get there. No matter how many times I tried to focus on him, on how good this felt, the nagging thoughts of guilt and shame crept in.

How could I lie here and let him do this to me when I was lying to him?

What was okay about my asking for this loving from him when I hid his son from him?

"Come back to me, Chloe," he said, sweet but rough as he added another finger.

I groaned at my tightness stretching around him. It drove more pleasure through me, but his words stalled me.

Come back to him? How many times did he think that over the years? How long had he wished for that? I knew he said it now, at this moment, because he could tell that I was getting distracted. He meant it as an order to focus on him, on this moment.

"I've lost too much time with you," he said as he left my pussy and crawled back up until he spooned me. "And I refuse to lose any more."

I sighed at the change of positions. He lifted my leg to drape over his as he thrust into me from behind. Twisting to lower his head, he latched his mouth over my nipple and sucked hard.

Again, he pushed me so close to coming. With every stroke of his big cock sliding in and out of me, he urged me that much closer to exploding in an intense orgasm. He coaxed me to come, to rupture and squeeze him, to milk him dry.

But once more, those gnawing thoughts and worries about how I'd wronged him ate at me.

"I want you to come for me, Chloe." He paired his gruff instruction with a slap on my ass.

I stiffened, holding my breath. He'd never done anything like this before. He'd never lifted a hand to me. Wes did, to hurt me. While the slap on my ass stung, it also felt... good.

"Chloe?" he asked, noticing my reaction.

"I..." I couldn't say it.

He didn't need me to explain. He rained another slap on my ass, that cheek exposed to the air with my leg draped over his. As the heat of the smack warmed my skin, he moved his fingers to my pussy. With his dick slid almost all the way back out, he felt around where we were connected, no doubt noticing how much more aroused I was.

"You like it?"

I nodded and thrust back against him. "More."

It shocked me, how much I liked him spanking me as he fucked me hard, but it was a different element that served to push me over the edge. He saw that I was distracted, and with a little bit of a kink to throw me off, I came so swiftly and so forcefully, he muffled my cries with kisses.

He followed me, flooding my pussy with his hot cum.

"Fuck, Chloe. I fucking love you," he growled against me. Holding me close, he repeated those words as he slowed his thrusts and slumped to the bed.

Caught in his hug, his dick so deep inside me, I replayed the words I never thought I'd hear again.

I love you.

I loved him too. I never stopped loving him. But until I could come clean and tell him that we had a son, I feared he wouldn't want to consider how deeply I'd feel for him.

19

FRANCO

By the time I caught my breath after coming so hard in Chloe, she was asleep. We lay there, tangled together in my bed, and she passed out.

"Long day?" I whispered aloud, amused that I'd literally fucked her so well that she passed out afterward. She was like that when we were younger, too, so into the act of making love that she became so sated and satisfied she drifted off afterward.

Proud that I could please her, I got up to clean off and then brought back a towel to clean her up too. She didn't stir, and I climbed back into bed to hold her. Sleeping with her in my arms was becoming my norm. She grounded me, and I appreciated being able to reunite with her like this. I tried not to dwell on the fact that she hadn't told me she loved me too. I said it in the heat of the moment, but I meant it. I would always mean it. Nothing she could do would prevent me from loving her.

Which worsened my concerns.

She'd been distracted, and I wanted to know why.

She'd been guarded earlier when I spoke about Dante, and I was eager to understand why.

Still, she kept things from me, and I was losing patience to get answers.

I closed my eyes, sighing as I breathed in a deep lungful of her scent. In the morning, I'd ask. Before anything else could get in the way, I would lie in bed with her and ask who she'd called that day. I wanted to be able to trust her. That if I asked, she'd reply. If I had to snoop and try to track her phone, it would be a clear sign of her being untrustworthy, which would hurt with how she already had my heart.

I woke up to the sound of my phone buzzing, though, and it seemed this morning wouldn't be the opportune time to talk with her about anything.

I grabbed the device from my nightstand and with bleary eyes as I woke up more, I read the texts from Romeo.

Goddammit.

It was always something, always another situation popping up, another fire to put out.

I slipped out of bed without waking Chloe. Hurrying to get dressed, I watched her sleep and considered what we talked about before the wedding. Her comment about Dante having a work-and-family balance. Yes, it was taxing to work for the Constella Family. Our jobs never stopped. The danger never slept. Someone else was always out there waiting to try to take what was ours.

But it wasn't any different from any other occupation. If Chloe and I had married years ago, she would've seen how I could fit her into my life, how she could've gone to school and had her own career if she wanted.

We were always busy. Sometimes, it felt more hectic than not, but we came together as a family and tackled this Mafia lifestyle together. If Chloe gave me—us—a chance, she'd see that. She already should be noticing how I could make her life better. With my love. With my protection. With my determination to remove the threat of her ex.

It was with that mindset that I headed into Dante's office.

"First day of your 'honeymoon' and this is what you get?" I joked as I brought my coffee in with me. On the walk down here, I filed through all the reports that the capos sent me.

"How bad is it?" Dante asked. He yawned from his seat behind his desk, but he didn't look too stressed. He didn't reply to my tease, and if anything, he seemed ready to go right back to bed after we talked.

Only Romeo was in, also on his phone and following up with what the capos sent in. I was technically the head of security for the organization, but that was more of a managerial role, of delegating who went where. Dante, Romeo, and Liam were all given the same shared intel, and I knew they had likely already skimmed through what was popping up overnight.

"Not that it *is* bad—for us," Dante added. "If Stefan Giovanni wants to hunt down and fight whoever else might have survived from the Domino Family, he can help himself to it." He rolled his eyes, punctuating his opinion on his former friend who'd turned shady.

That was what the messages were about—reports of Stefan and his capos attacking a hideout where some of Donny Domino's survivors were reported to be lurking and staying on the down-low. The Constella soldiers raised the alarm because of how close it happened to some of the capos' homes.

"We don't have a part in this," Dante reiterated. "We don't need to have a part in a single fucking thing Stefan wants to get up to."

Romeo nodded. "If any Domino men survived the attack from the Devil's Brothers, I vote for letting the Giovannis take them out."

"Yeah," I agreed. "And then the Giovannis and Devil's Brothers can cancel each other out next."

"Oh." Romeo looked up. "Did you hear that Gunner is the Prez now?"

He glanced at Dante, who groaned.

"Fucking bikers. I don't have the time or patience to dick around and care about whatever roles and policies the fucking MC men use. They are insignificant in terms of the long-standing power we've held as the Constella force—or other crime families in the city."

"Well, until they're all dead or powerless," Romeo said, "it seems that Gunner is now the self-proclaimed leader of the Devil's Brothers. As of last night, at least."

I was mildly curious. We were on the same page of letting our enemies kill each other off, no matter how long it would feel like a waiting game. "What about Reaper? Is he dead?"

"Dead or dying." Romeo shrugged. "It sounds like they damn near burned down their clubhouse with infighting."

"Then fuck them. Let them all rot in hell," Dante said as he stood. He was still angry, rightly so, about the motorcycle gang. They kidnapped Nina from him and tried to trespass to destroy his home here. I couldn't blame him for his attitude toward them.

"I'm going to start my honeymoon with my wife." As he walked to the door, he looked at us one at a time. "But remain on alert. We will monitor this activity but not get involved."

I nodded once in acknowledgment.

"Keep the soldiers and guards on high alert," he ordered before he went.

Romeo and I stayed in the office, finishing our coffee and replying to the capos and men who reported in for updates on orders.

"Even though we need to be focused on this activity, we can't let the situation with Wes Morrison fall to the back burner," I reminded him.

"Correct." He sighed, then rubbed his face. "But so far, he's hiding rather well."

As a man in a position like his, that made sense. He was a public figure, which meant he'd take caution with anyone being able to track him or stalk *him*.

"He's not the first corrupt cop or political figure we've taken down," I said.

"Has Chloe said anything else about him?" he asked. "Or the shooting?"

I shook my head. "No." *She isn't talking about much of anything now.*

"What's that look for?" he asked, frowning at me.

I cringed. "I feel like she's hiding something from me."

"That pertains to the shooting? Or Wes?"

I shrugged. "No. Yes?" I was confident that if she knew something that would be a security issue, she'd come clean. "Ten years is a long time. She hasn't been in my life all that while, and I know she's lived her life."

"A lot could happen in a decade."

"Yeah. But the longer she's here, the closer we get, I have to wonder if she wants to stay."

"If she wants to stay this time," he clarified.

Chloe wasn't someone coming into the family for the first time. Dante, Romeo, and Eva all remembered her from before. They accepted her back then, and they weren't opposed to welcoming her into the family again now. I didn't fault Romeo for being suspicious of her, given the circumstances she'd come into our lives again, as a witness to an attack.

"If she doesn't..." he said carefully.

"I don't want to think about that." I shot him a hard look. "She's it for me. She has always been the one for me. If she doesn't feel the same about me, I'll spend the rest of my life with her holding half of my heart."

"Has she talked about why she ran before?"

I shook my head, hating how secretive and guarded she was. I'd *never* given her a reason to doubt me. I'd never given her an example of how I wouldn't stand by her and support her.

"It's got to be her parents. Her fear of sticking with us despite their being all self-righteous and telling her that we're bad people. Criminals."

He rolled his eyes. "To the point they'd send Morrison after her and try to bring her home to them?"

I nodded. "You know how controlling they were." He'd never met them, but we talked. Even Chloe told him how hard they were to please when she hung out with me and Romeo when he visited.

"She's their only daughter and they wanted her to be the good girl, the sweet, upstanding citizen of a wholesome small town. Not with a Mafia 'gangster' and living a life of crime in the city." Now I had to roll my eyes. It was so stupid, so closed-minded.

"What I don't get is how she was all for moving here with you when you'd further your training. From what I remember, she made it sound like she wanted to go against her parents' wishes and choose you."

I grunted. I remembered that as well. "Something had to have changed to make her reconsider." By running off to college far away, without telling me goodbye, it seemed she was all talk about wanting a future with me.

"What, though?" Romeo asked. "What could have happened to make her change her mind?"

I didn't know. For so long, I'd assumed it was the same old. The issue of her parents being so vehemently against the idea of Chloe living with me or marrying me. They despised me when we dated, and they never lightened up on their opinions of me no matter how much Chloe argued I wasn't a horrible person.

"Whatever prompted her to change her mind, it was stronger than any feelings she had for me."

He watched me stand. "And what of her feelings now?"

Last night, they all saw me with Chloe and how much of a couple we were, dancing and eating like we were at a real wedding as each other's date.

"Are they strong enough to make her stay this time?" Romeo asked.

I shrugged, hating that I didn't know the answer to that. In my arms, I could swear that she loved me as fiercely as I did her. Until she could explain why she left and stayed away, though, I refused to claim that I knew anything about her sentiments. I was sick of assuming that I was good enough to fight for, that I was worthy of her love for good.

As I left him with that question, I wondered what it would take to get the final answers from her without pushing her too hard.

Back in the recess of my mind, I feared the worst.

Maybe she'd never feel as deeply about me.

There was a chance I'd never be deemed worthy of her love forever.

And I hated that she could render me so powerless as to need her love to feel whole. To feel complete.

20

CHLOE

My self-loathing pushed me to get out of bed. The longer I kept the truth about Caleb from Franco, the worse I felt.

Instead of lying in bed and rehearsing how I could tell him once and for all, I wondered where he'd gone. I was alone in his room, but I felt like a trespasser, an imposter of a lover to be here when I was actively deceiving him by not revealing that he was a father.

I got up and headed back to my guest room that I slept in the night before. After I dressed in another change of the borrowed clothes Eva and Tessa provided for me during my stay, I sought Franco.

Forgoing breakfast, I settled for a cup of iced coffee. If I ate anything, it might come back up. That was how nervous I was. The little bit of a conversation I overheard from the men on the other side of the kitchen put me on edge too. They were guards, more men I didn't know, but their mention of people fighting in Brooklyn made me think of Caleb, who was staying there for now.

For now. In a couple of days, I would have to put an end to my stay here. I would need to go pick him up from his spring break vacation with Ethan.

I had to go back to real life, the one in which I was a single mother determined to hide from her stalker of an ex.

I had stayed under the illusion of being here in the lap of luxury and free to reconnect with the man I loved and missed.

This was it. The moment had come. I had to tell Franco and I had to go back to Caleb.

Franco had shown me nothing but security. He had been patient and so tender with me, letting me into his life without any exceptions and conditions. I had no reason not to come clean. No excuses.

Just do it. Tell him.

I resolved to, no matter how hard it would be.

When I finally found him in the massive home gym in the mansion, I was thankful that no one else was working out with him. Among the many pieces of equipment and mirrored walls, he was building up a sweat on his own.

"Chloe." He grinned around a strained expression as he set a bar with weights back on a rack. "Over here."

I swallowed, nervous, and approached. "I see that." Crossing my arms felt like a defensive posture, but I wanted the comfort of something like a hug.

Looking him up and down, I couldn't help but smile. He was always so strong and ripped, oozing testosterone and masculinity. He was a buff gym junkie, but not with the bulkiness of someone who got so strong for the sake of looking good. His fitness was tied to his job. As a capo for Dante's organization, Franco was expected to always be primed to fight, run, and defend.

This man would never fail to get a reaction out of me.

I stole this moment to look my fill. His sweaty hair, the blond tips dripping wet. His chiseled, lean features showing the tautness of his face. All the way down over the bulging muscles in his shoulders, those strong arms that held me so well.

I sighed at the sight of his hard pecs decorated with so many tattoos. Every ridge and dip of his abs, every slab of hardness defined and shiny under the glistening sheen of sweat.

"Chloe." He grunted my name with that hit of a needy growl, and I swore I was aroused just like that. No matter the state of my mind and how anxious I was to talk to him, I was overwhelmed with immediate lust.

For him. Always for him. Something about this man called to me. His soul, the promise of his sexy body, his commanding grip.

"You keep looking at me like that, sweetheart, and I'm going to forget what I came here to do."

He stalked toward me, his gaze predatory but playful.

I shook my head slightly, wrenching myself out of this haze of lust. "Me too." I came here for something specific. I had to talk to him. I came here to talk about Caleb and break the news that he was a father.

But I overheard the guards near the kitchen when I grabbed my coffee. I didn't know who the Giovannis were, but they were fighting someone in the Brooklyn area—where Caleb was with Ethan. I trusted that man to keep him safe. That reminder of Caleb, though, prompted me to get to it and tell Franco already.

"You don't like the way I'm looking at you?" he teased, coming up to me and walking me back to the wall of mirrors.

"I really like the way you're looking at me," I replied before he kissed me so hard I grew dizzy.

"Like I want to eat you up?" he taunted, licking a path down my neck. He thrust my loose shorts down and slid his hand to my pussy.

"Oh, shit." I gasped at the push of his fingers into my sex. The rough stroke and firm pressure were exactly what I needed and wanted with how quickly he turned me on like this.

"Like I want to drive my cock into your cunt?"

I moaned as I brought him back for a hard kiss.

"Like that?" he taunted, adding his thumb to rub at my clit.

"Fuck. Franco." I caught my breath, or tried to. "I wanted to talk to you."

"Hmm." He sucked at my neck. "Then talk. Go ahead and see how long you can think while I do this."

I whined, grabbing his forearm to slow him down. I was already overwhelmed with the need to come, but I strained to focus.

I told myself last night that I'd be greedy one last time and enjoy what he offered. Purely filthy, hot, and wild sex. That was supposed to be the last time I let my body betray me, the last time I would cave and give in to the pressure of wanting him so badly that I'd combust.

"Seriously," I protested breathily between kisses. He was far stronger than me. If he wanted to move his arm, he would, but he humored me, letting me think that I could keep his hand in place as he continued to finger me.

He didn't reply, kissing me again and groaning as he pinned me to the wall of mirrors. They had to be fogging up with the heat and moisture of him so sweaty and warming me up with the idea of sex.

"I want to talk to you." I closed my eyes tighter, willing myself to resist him. It was so hard. *He* was hard. I felt the hardness of his erection prodding against me as he caged me against the wall.

"I'm always here for you. You can tell me anything."

If he didn't say that in such a seductive, panted whisper, it wouldn't've hit harder. It would've sounded like a sincere claim that I could believe in. Right now, it seemed that we were on the fast track to a hot, quick fuck.

"I want to talk to you about something important."

He growled, kissing up my neck and rubbing his erection against me. The full-body grind turned me on more. I didn't care if he was sweaty and filthy. I relished the promise of his hard muscles grinding against me, his hands gripping me so tightly.

"Everything you have to say is important to me, Chloe. *You* are important to me. You always have been."

I winced at his words. He'd stand by them with what he knew about me now. Once I told him my biggest secret, he might want to walk that statement back and pretend it wasn't true.

"Please, just let me tell you—"

His phone rang, cutting through the quiet. Over the panted breaths we shared in here, riled up from the potential quickie we'd embarked on having, his phone rang and rang.

"Dammit."

He gritted his teeth, backing up from me quickly. "Stay right there." Pointing at me, he kept me in place.

My mouth hung open. I was so startled by how quickly we were interrupted. After his hot body was pressed flush to mine, I felt the absence of his warmth the second he peeled back.

"Um." I licked my lips and nodded. "Yeah."

"I need to take this. We've had security issues," he said, backpedaling toward the shelf he put his phone on. It seemed like he couldn't take his eyes off me. The further he backed up, the more intense the longing in his gaze got.

"The Constella forces keeping an eye on some Giovanni guys in Brooklyn." I nodded. "I, um, I overheard some men in the kitchen."

"We live in a dangerous world, but that doesn't mean I can't have you in it too," he said as he reached for his phone.

I furrowed my brow as his odd line sank in. He probably said that because of how I referenced the family-work balance yesterday, when I mentioned that Dante must have struggled to be both a single dad to Romeo and to run the entire Mafia family.

I shook my head. That wasn't a worry. That never crossed my mind, that Franco wouldn't be able to be a partner for me now that we'd reunited. Back when I found out that I was pregnant with Caleb, I stressed about it. I was gravely concerned that Franco wouldn't have had the time to be a father to a newborn when he was just getting committed to his career. It played a big part in why I left.

"Liam," Franco answered on speaker. He stared at me and ran his hand through his hair. "What's going on?"

"I'm not sure."

Franco furrowed his brow. "Talk to me."

"I'm off today," Liam said, "but I think something has come up that we need to follow up on. I know Romeo was teaming up with you on this while I focused on other things, but this is too weird of a coincidence to ignore."

"Go on." His tone suggested that he was impatient, both to reclaim this moment we were sharing and to get to the bottom of whatever Liam was talking about.

"I've got this friend, someone I used to work with. He's into, uh, private services."

Franco nodded. "Okay."

"He called because he's aware that I have connections from working with you. He reached out to me just to shoot the shit, you know, just to stay in touch, but he mentioned that he was annoyed about some asshole hanging around his place."

Franco made a face at me and rolled his hand, as though wishing Liam would get to the point already.

"Said this guy is harassing people in his building, asking questions and being nosy. You know? That sort of thing."

"What about it?" Franco asked.

"He mentioned his name was Morrison."

My blood turned cold. I swore my heart skipped a beat. Franco went still, staring at me with a frigid expression of shock.

"Morrison?" he asked.

"Yeah. Morrison, same name as Chloe's stalker, right? I guess it's a common enough name, but I think it seems sort of odd. It's worth checking out, wouldn't you say?"

Franco nodded, hurrying through the gym to grab a towel to wipe off his bare chest. "Definitely."

"I've got a car ready. If you want to go—"

"Yes. I'll be out front in five minutes." He disconnected the call as he jogged to me. "Wait for me." He pulled me in close for a hard, fast kiss, and I sagged against the mirrored wall when he let me go.

"Wait. I—"

Too late. He lifted a hand in a wave and darted out of the room.

I was left behind, stuck with all these trapped words and confessions stuck in my throat.

The idea of his rushing off to find Wes scared me. He'd kill him. There was not a chance in hell that Franco would let him live. While I didn't want to think about the grisly details, I tried not to dwell on the fact that it would be happening. Soon. In a normal world, I should've been worried and alarmed, knowing about a murder waiting to happen. With what Wes did to me, stalking me and threatening me, though, I knew better than to wish for a different outcome.

That didn't make me a bad person. I refused to accept that.

However, I felt like the scummiest coward and liar. Standing here all alone with my secrets, I hated myself a little more for *still* not coming clean about having Franco's son and hiding him.

As soon as he's back. I have *to tell him. No more excuses.*

21

FRANCO

"It's so close to where the Giovannis started up a fight," I commented once I joined Liam in the car and left the mansion. I did another double-take at the address on the navigation, the location where Liam's former military buddy lived in Brooklyn.

"Yeah. I noticed that too." Liam concentrated on the road as he sped away. "But I don't see how that'd be relevant."

"Who is this friend again?" I asked. I felt like I should've known this.

"Ethan Koone. We served together overseas. He retired a few years ago and sort of started up his, uh, own business."

"In what field or industry?"

Liam glanced at me. "Killing. He's a contracted hitman."

I raised my brows. "No shit."

"Yeah." He shrugged. "I spoke with him a little bit when I was debating whether I should join the Constella forces."

I laughed once, wryly. "I'd say a hitman for hire would sway the black-and-white areas of your moral compass."

He nodded. "He suggested that I work for him, actually, as partners. But that was right before I found out about Olivia, and I couldn't do that then."

"Of course not. And you're one of us." I checked my gun and slid it back into my holster. I didn't take the time to shower after leaving Chloe so horny and needy in the gym. It killed me to leave her hanging like that—to give myself blue balls in walking away from her—but I had to. A lead on Wes Morrison was nothing to pass up on.

"I most certainly am. But Ethan's a good guy. Older, but still fit and with it. He usually watches his grandson over longer breaks. I think the kid moved around a lot, but he got a pen pal through some program and they're best friends. Ethan said he was at home with Brent, his grandson, and this friend who's visiting, but if he were alone, he'd look into this nosy guy himself."

"Will he have surveillance footage we could take a look at if this guy isn't there when we arrive?" I checked the time on the dashboard, grimacing when I realized how many minutes had passed already. If Wes would be a hard guy to track down, we'd need to move fast before he hid again.

"Absolutely," Liam answered.

On the drive there, I tried not to think back to the moment I'd been interrupted from having with Chloe. When she showed up, I thought it would be my chance to ask her about what she was hiding. After we shared those heated looks, though, we were both goners.

It was too damn easy to be tempted with her sexy body. One look was all it took. The moment we touched, the second we kissed, it was damn near impossible to resist each other.

But we had to talk. Not only according to me, either. She said she had something important on her mind to share with me, and I hated that we'd been interrupted. While it was hard to keep our hands and mouths off each other, we had a solid connection beyond raw, carnal sex.

It was the worst time to be interrupted, but catching Wes was crucial—for that shooting investigation and to go after Chloe's biggest threat.

Before long, we pulled up to the apartment where Ethan lived.

"Ready?" Liam asked, scanning the area.

We were both packing, but there was not a chance we'd risk going in guns blazing. We had to handle this carefully, especially since it wasn't in Constella territory. It wasn't really anyone's area. Long ago, the Cartel operated around here, but it was more like an unclaimed, complicated area of the city.

I nodded. "After you."

Liam led the way up to Ethan's floor. He knocked, and we waited outside. "Ethan? It's me."

No one answered, and I felt tension knotting up on my shoulders and over my upper back. Bracing for a hit, I stood off to the side and continued to look back and forth, watching out for Liam.

"Ethan?" Liam tried again, knocking louder.

He frowned, glancing down at his phone. "Huh."

"What?"

"He says to smile. We're on camera."

I frowned. "Where is he?"

"Upstairs. He rents two separate units out."

I raised my brows, spotting the camera hidden overhead. The tiny lens fit in well with the molding. "Huh is right. He's a paranoid bastard, then, isn't he?"

Liam nodded. "I can't blame him after the shit we lived through and saw during our tours." Tipping his head toward the stairwell, he indicated for me to follow him through there.

Upstairs, just one more level up, we repeated it all. He knocked, and I remained on a lookout.

Ethan answered the door quickly. He was just as I expected, older but trim and fit. He looked like he could kick ass, but he also had a general lack of a unique appearance. This man was likely very skilled at slipping in and out of tricky situations in his hitman assignments that he accepted.

"Liam. Good to see you." He stepped back, letting us enter.

"This is my good friend, Franco," Liam said. "Franco, this is Ethan."

Ethan gave me a quick once-over as he gestured for me to enter. His scrutiny was brief, but I had no doubt he could size me up well in that glance. "Good to meet you."

Liam could've identified me better than that. As his supervisor. As a colleague. As an acquaintance. This wasn't a business call, though. This wasn't an official business meeting but checking in with his old friend. I didn't care about formalities in a situation like this. All I cared about was clearing out this "coincidence" of someone named Morrison snooping around here and being a nuisance.

"He slipped away," Ethan grumbled as he shut the door. He shook his head while he engaged the multiple locks. "I got him on the cameras, so I can show ya. But he just ran off."

Dammit!

Ethan noticed my cringe. "Mrs. Gehring down the hall got him kicked out. He was asking around by the laundromat downstairs about where the playground was. She got all in his face, shouting at him for being a pedophile and creep. He's been hanging around for a couple of days, but that's the first time he started asking around. Fucker." He shook his head, disgusted. "If I knew one of those sick assholes were hanging around here, I wouldn't have hesitated to kill him. I had the boys out and about at the museum and the park, so I didn't hear about this until after I ran into her in the hallway on the way to get my mail."

"I can't stand sick fuckers like that."

"What got me calling you and asking for help was if he came back," Ethan said. "Mrs. Gehring said that she threatened to call the cops on him and he laughed. *Laughed.* Like it wouldn't have mattered to him if she did."

Seeing that Wes Morrison used to be a lawman himself, that didn't surprise me.

"She damn near beat him with her purse, and his wallet fell out. That was how her niece got his name. Little Beatrice swooped down and picked through his wallet before he could snatch it back. That's how we got his name. I haven't run a search on him yet, but I will. I just figure with your new, uh..." He glanced at me. "Your new employment and connection, you might be interested in killing a corrupt cop."

We weren't vigilantes at large. We weren't crusading to act as another law enforcement agency, going after the sickos in the world. Our loyalty was to our family. But Wes was on our radar. Because he targeted Chloe, we damn well did want to kill him. His act of ordering an attack on our building hadn't won him any favors, either. If he was behind that hit, he'd pay for the damages on our property and for killing any members of the organization, like Manny and Suzie.

"His name's Wes Morrison," a boy said.

He appeared in the hallway with another short boy.

"Go on back in the living room, boys," Ethan said.

"But you don't have to run a search or look him up," the blond said.

I narrowed my eyes at him, struck with a sense of recognition. I'd never seen him before, but he looked familiar. Like... a younger version of me.

"Go on, Caleb. This conversation is for me and—"

I stepped forward, unable to tear my attention from the kid. "*Caleb?*"

No. No fucking way. Of all the names this kid could've had, it had to be the one I swore I heard Chloe say when she was in that first room. The person she called as soon as she got her tampered burner phone back.

"*Caleb?*" I was rooted in shock, so confused and stunned by what had to be true.

"Yes." Ethan frowned, volleying his focus between me and this boy.

Liam did the same, looking from me to him. "Oh... *shit.*"

It seemed that he'd made the same connection that I had. The tall, slim boy had my eyes. His nose looked like mine too. But his hair was like his mother's.

"Yeah, I'm Caleb," he said, sticking his chin up defiantly.

My heart raced. My chest felt too tight. Panicked and feeling like the rug had been pulled from beneath my feet, I gaped at this boy who had to be related to me.

"That's my grandson's friend," Ethan said. "He's been staying with us over his spring break while his mom starts a new job and gets settled in."

"Oh, *shit*." Liam repeated it with more conviction.

Starting a new job at a deli, I bet. And settling into a new home in New York somewhere, since she was always on the run from her stalker ex.

I couldn't look away, more shocked than ever before.

"I know who *you* are too, Mister." Caleb narrowed his eyes, suspicious and untrusting of me despite claiming to recognize me.

"What the…? You know who *I* am?" I pointed at myself unnecessarily. He was just as locked in this surprised stare-down as I was. He had yet to look away from me, checking me out as though he doubted I was real and here.

"Yeah. I've seen lots of pictures of you. I never met you before, but yeah, Mister, I know exactly who you are, Mr. Franco."

Oh, fuck.

Denial could no longer work. It was my instinct to think it couldn't be possible. That my eyes were playing tricks on me. That this kid just happened to look like me. Not that he was mine.

"My mom always showed me pictures of you." He crossed his arms.

"Your mom—" I choked on my dry throat and strained to swallow. "Your mom showed you pictures of *me*."

"Yeah. So I'd grow up knowing I had a daddy and what he looked like." Caleb frowned at me, still so wary of my showing up here.

Daddy.

This boy, this kid, he thought I was his father.

The idea that I had a son nearly knocked me over. I felt blown away, so clueless and floundering for a shred of reality as I knew and recognized it.

I was a father?

I had a *son*?

As I steadied my breaths and stared at Caleb, I felt my heart cracking and swelling. I was a mess, unsure what to think or how to feel. Elation was my first reaction, but just as swiftly, anger.

I fumed while I wanted to rejoice that I had a son. I seethed, combatting the wonderful marvel of knowing I was a father.

I knew Chloe had been keeping something from me.

But I hadn't counted on something like finding out she'd hidden our son from me for years.

22

CHLOE

I was so close to telling Franco about Caleb. So close, but so far.

We distracted each other with lust, but that was no excuse.

Then Liam's call about a lead on Wes came in, but that wasn't something I could control.

As I left the gym and avoided my room, I felt antsy and unsure what to do. Until I could woman up and tell Franco my big secret, until I could finally tell him why I ran away all those years ago, this tense, prickling sense of shame and anxiety would continue to consume me.

"Chloe?" Tessa asked when I passed her in the kitchen. Again. I thought grabbing a water bottle would give me something to do, but I was still on edge. I ended up pacing back to put it back, not in the mood to eat or drink anything.

I faced her as Eva came into the room too.

"Are you all right?"

I shrugged, then hugged myself.

"For God's sake, Tessa," Eva drawled dryly. "Of course, she's not all right. Look at her."

I winced at Eva.

"What's going on?"

I heaved in a deep breath. I still couldn't tell them that I was the mother of Franco's son. He had the right to learn that before them.

But I couldn't blow them off and lie poorly that nothing was wrong. Like Eva pointed out, they saw on my face how something had to be terribly not right.

"I..." I heaved out a deep breath, latching on to the other thing bugging me. "Franco and Liam left to go after Wes."

Eva nodded. "Yeah..."

"And I know that means they will kill him." I swallowed hard. "I've never... I haven't been involved in someone's death before. That's not something I ever wanted to be involved with."

"Whoa. No. Hold on." Tessa shook her head. "You are *not* at fault here."

"You're a victim," Eva said. "Wes brought this upon himself. And he will answer for *his* actions."

"But—"

Tessa took my hand. "Listen. It *is* weird. I struggled with it a little bit myself. The whole concept of knowing someone is going to die, to be killed, by a man you trust. And love." She raised her brows. "Right? You love Franco?"

"I've loved Franco my whole life. Before I left him ten years ago, during that time apart, and now."

"Okay. So..." She winced a bit. "It takes some adjustment. Because this isn't a normal way of processing justice. If you're not born into the Mafia life"—she gestured at Eva—"there's a learning curve. An adjustment."

"But it feels so bizarre..." I winced, wishing I could get over it. "Back then, I didn't see Franco as a killer. I saw him as my boyfriend. Now, I *know* he's a killer. I know he killed that man who chased me to the hotel after they shot up the deli. Liam too. I'm grateful they removed the dangerous men hunting me down."

Eva shrugged. "It's the same thing, Chloe. Franco will kill your stalker to protect you."

"Well, that and because he had the deli shot up, a Constella business," Tessa added.

Eva shook her head. "He's going to avenge her. Because he loves her."

Tessa nodded. "You get used to it."

I huffed. "The idea of them killing people? I think I might be too much of a pacifist for this."

"Nonsense," Nina said as she entered the room.

"How is it nonsense?" I asked.

"Because they kill to keep us safe," she replied. "Like the time Dante killed the men who kidnapped me and almost gang raped me. No cops would've delivered justice like that."

Tessa chimed in as well. "Romeo killed the men who *did* rape me." She sucked in a deep breath as though it was hard for her to say that out loud.

"And Liam killed countless enemies overseas when he was in the military," Eva said.

"We will help you," Tessa said. "We all stick together, even us women as the men keep us safe."

I smiled at her, appreciating her kindness. "Thanks. I… I needed that."

"Anytime you want to talk, we're here," Nina said.

Dante and Romeo entered the room, glancing at us and pausing in whatever they were speaking about.

"Is… everything okay?" Dante asked, looking at Nina first. His brows were raised.

"Yeah. Everything's okay." Eva nodded. "Or it will be."

Romeo looked at me and opened then closed his mouth. As though he had something to suggest otherwise. He swallowed whatever he had to say, though, because the front door burst open.

And my son ran inside.

"Caleb?" I blinked quickly, unable to believe my eyes. "Caleb!"

It'd only been several days since I dropped him off at Ethan's apartment. But it was the longest we'd ever been apart.

My baby!

I dropped to my knees and held my arms out as he launched at me. Nothing else mattered. All the other details of the room faded into a meaningless blur as I focused on my sweet little boy running into my arms.

"I missed you, Mommy."

He crashed into me, and I didn't hesitate to hold him to me. His small arms squeezed me tight, and I closed my eyes at the firm hug he gave me. I tightened my embrace and buried my face against his neck. The first deep scent of him somehow calmed my heart. My soul was full, and I knew that everything truly would be all right now.

Caleb was my miracle. My savior. My reason to live. He was proof that love always prevailed despite the wicked hardships that were thrown at me, at us.

I went to the extremes to keep him alive and with me, and I would never, *ever* regret a decision that I made in the name of love for my son.

He was the reason I would never tell Franco that I regretted leaving him the way I had. Caleb was the proof that I had to run from his father in order to keep us both alive and well.

"I missed you, too," I told him.

I felt the rise of his cheek against mine, that little roundness pushing up with his smile at my words. I was everything he had, and he was all I thought that I had. For his whole life, that was it. We had each other, and I fought every time to keep that true.

I clung to him, letting him hold me tight. After so many days away from him, it felt too damn good and right to have him in my arms again. Separation anxiety was a wicked beast, but when I was also suffering from other fears and threats, it had me worried that I'd never see him again.

When I feared the shooters at the deli, and then when they chased me all the way to the motel, I worried that Caleb would be orphaned, that he'd lose me.

When I came here and fell deeper under the spell of loving Franco again, I worried that I wouldn't be able to explain without blowing up both of our worlds.

I had to now. Letting myself calm down with the reassurance of my happy, healthy son in my arms, I slowly returned to the moment that everyone else was locked in here.

They had to be so confused. So surprised. Caleb's dashing in here was a huge shock. I felt the burn of all their stares on me, but I couldn't focus on them. I couldn't spend my energy on explaining that I was a mother and this darling boy was my son.

The only person I owed answers to was his father.

Franco.

If Caleb was here...

Confusion kicked in now. I held Caleb close, letting his presence soothe me, but I racked my brain for how in the world he'd just appeared here.

"Liam," Eva said from the side of the room.

Wait. Liam is back. That means Franco must be too. And if they came here with Caleb...

"Oh, God..." I mumbled. I was lagging horribly, delayed in my reaction time with Caleb showing up unexpectedly like this. My confusion lingered, but as I made the connection that Liam and Franco must have brought Caleb here...

"Mommy, I met Daddy!"

Oh, fuck. Oh, fuck me. My heart raced again. This time, not in elation and joy at seeing my son, but in trepidation and dread.

"You... did?" I opened my eyes, facing the music.

Franco entered the house. He stood in the foyer, staring at me with such an unreadable expression. I sensed his pain, the anger he tried to keep inside.

He was furious, and rightly so.

My big moment of truth was here, all right. And because I waited too long to tell him a thing, it was all exploding in a huge, chaotic mess.

I stood on shaky knees. My stomach dropped, sinking with all the knots of shame, guilt, and anxiety.

I knew I should have told him sooner. I should've come clean immediately, but nothing about this was simple. Not a thing was cut and dry, easy to determine.

I felt so lost since the moment the deli was shot up. Now, my mistakes were catching up to me.

"Look, Mommy," Caleb said as he tugged my hand and pointed. "He's right there. He and his buddy came to tell Wes to get lost."

I widened my eyes, looking at Franco for confirmation that Wes was gone.

Liam cleared his throat. "Unfortunately, Mr. Morrison wasn't around."

Caleb sighed, dejected. "Next time, then."

I frowned at my son and squeezed his hand, prompting me to face me. "What do you mean, next time?"

"He came to Brent's apartment all week. I saw him and made sure he couldn't see me. Like you taught me."

"Did you tell Mr. Ethan?" I asked, so pissed that danger tagged after my son. When would it ever end?

It will end when Franco kills him, that's when.

"No. Because I knew if Wes was looking for me, he couldn't be bugging you or looking for you."

Oh, Jesus. I hugged him to my side. This sweet, protective boy, trying to watch out for me when it was my job to take care of him.

Looking at Franco, I sucked in my lower lip and strained to explain. All the words I rehearsed didn't come.

"Is Caleb my son?" he asked.

His voice was dry and dull, monotone, as if he were numb.

"The math seems about right," he added.

I inhaled a deep breath and stared right back into the eyes of the man I loved. The man who I hoped would love me after I broke his heart all over again as I confessed my darkest secret.

"Caleb?" Dante's voice cut through the thick tension in the air.

"That's your name?" he asked.

"Yes, sir," my son answered. "Who's asking?"

He chuckled. "Yeah, the attitudes match, Franco," he said quietly. "My name is Dante, Caleb. Do you like to swim?"

"I love to swim!" Caleb furrowed his brow. "But isn't it kind of cold to be swimming outside yet?"

"Come check out this pool back here, then."

Caleb tightened his grip on my hand. "My mom says I can't follow strangers anywhere."

"He's not a stranger," I told my son.

"Yeah. He's my dad," Romeo said, joining in Dante's efforts to distract my son.

"Daddy!" Olivia said as she ran toward Liam. She'd just come in the room with a nanny, but she ran too fast and tripped.

Caleb rushed out to catch her, and they both tumbled so goofily that they ended up laughing.

"Good catch, Caleb," Liam said as he scooped up his giggling daughter. "If your mom's cool with it, I bet Olivia here would love to have a friend more her size to share the pool with."

"Can I, Mommy?"

I nodded, grateful for their distracting him from what would be a very, very difficult conversation.

23

FRANCO

One by one, the others filed out of the living room. They pitched in to help Caleb to the pool, seeming to see that I needed a private conversation with the mother of my child.

My son.

Caleb, who was so excited to swim, quick to help a falling toddler, and smart to question Dante.

The boy was already making me proud, and I'd only known him for an hour.

"Is he my son?" I asked Chloe.

She sighed, hesitant to face me, and looked around the room. "Can we have this conversation somewhere more private?"

"Answer me." My anger swarmed within me, coursing through my veins until I was certain I had to be shaking with rage. "Please," I added curtly. "Is Caleb my son?"

"He is."

I wouldn't have believed her if she said he wasn't. He looked like me. Acted like me. And his age made sense. If I did all the math and double-checked the addition, Chloe was pregnant with Caleb when she left.

With that realization sinking in, my fury faded and hurt rushed in. Pain nearly knocked me to my knees, and my heart cracked all over again.

"How could you hide this from me?" I shook my head, thinking back over this week that we'd shared. Every time we had sex. Those nights we shared in bed. Even when we talked about parenthood at Dante and Nina's wedding. She had many chances to come clean and tell me, but she hadn't, and that was more salt on the wound.

"How could you be so manipulative and deceiving?"

"I can explain—"

"Why?" I roared, fisting my hands. "How could you? All this time." I shook my head, needing something to make sense about this. "All these days you've been here with me again. How could you ever say that you love me and keep this from me?"

I staggered a step toward her, wishing I could shake sense into her.

But she doesn't. She didn't reply that she loved me that night I told her.

"I can explain." She winced as she took a seat. "And I can explain why I will never tell you that I regret leaving you back then the way I did. I had to." She swallowed as she hunched over, her elbows on her thighs, her hands wringing together with her fingers turning white at the knuckles. She was tense and coiling in, but she powered on.

"I had to leave to save him."

"What?" I paced in front of the couch she sat on, too wired up to stay still.

"I was trapped."

"Not by me!" I shouted.

She shook her head. "No. You didn't trap me." She whooshed out a deep breath, as if she were bracing for a long speech. "My parents tried to force me to have an abortion. The week before graduation, I took a test when I missed my period. It was positive, and I was so shocked, I didn't think straight to hide the test in my garbage. My mother must have either snooped in the trash or the housekeeper found it and told her, but she confronted me, telling me under no uncertain terms that I was to abort the baby. Because it was yours."

I rubbed my hand over my mouth, fighting the need to roar.

"She threatened to take my allowance. My car. My trust fund. Everything that was 'mine'. So I said fine. I was worried about it all—having a baby so young—and I wanted to tell you. But you were away for training and I wouldn't see you until after graduation."

I remembered it well. She was only going to the ceremony to appease her parents. She'd already graduated ahead of time the midterm before, already meeting her requirements with a perfect GPA, but her parents wanted her to walk and get her diploma with the rest of her class. Our plan was that I'd pick her up from graduation and drive her here to the city. Where she could start a future with me.

Only, she was never there. She'd already left.

The week I was in training was rough, and I hadn't had cell reception.

"She tricked me, driving me to an abortion clinic, and it was so scary, Franco. She walked me inside. The nurses were so firm. They wouldn't listen to me. I... I..."

"What?" I frowned at her.

"I punched one of the nurses so I could run out of there. I ran. But I didn't get far. They had the cops find my car and bring me back home. I was so desperate to tell you, but I knew that your cell reception would be spotty. I almost called Dante, the number you gave me for him, but I was scared that my parents were listening in on my calls.

"The day before graduation, I was kidnapped. They hired someone to kidnap me." She gestured at her hands. "They cuffed me." She pointed at her mouth. "Gagged me."

"Fuck, Chloe. *Fuck this!*" I couldn't ever hate her parents more than I did at this minute. They weren't parents. They were closed-minded assholes.

"The men who kidnapped me brought me to another abortion clinic. My mother was waiting there with these thugs they hired. She said she'd be damned if she'd let our family be tainted with a bastard from a Mafia criminal."

I shook my head, vibrating with rage.

"I was terrified, so I got desperate and lied. I said it wasn't yours, that some football player at school knocked me up and that was why you and I broke up. They didn't know that you were at a specialized training and unreachable that week. I think I figured they assumed we broke up. And I tried to spin it like that. That you weren't around that week because I got knocked up by someone else and you were mad." She shook her head sadly. "She didn't believe me. She ordered them to take me back into a room and abort the baby. But I..." She drew in a deep breath. "But I resisted. I fought and fought, so furious and scared. A nurse helped me, breaking her orders, and helped me get out of the room. And that was when I ran."

It destroyed me to envision this. The fear she had to have faced. The determination she had to find and keep our baby.

"I went to Santa Fe because it was the furthest from home, and I prayed that my parents would assume that the abortion had gone through. The nurse said she'd lie and cover for me."

I shook with anger. That she went through this. That she suffered at all. Her parents had taken it too far.

"I couldn't go to you. It was too close to home. I was terrified that they'd find me and have more cops look for me somewhere near you. You were a place and a person they could use to find me through. I gave birth at the college's vet clinic, trusting a classmate who knew a few faculty members to hide it. I paid someone to lie on his birth certificate so it wouldn't be tied to me. I had to hide him from my parents, Franco. From the world. And so, I was a single mother. I worked and studied. I had to drop out when it was too hard to manage it all."

"And Wes?"

She sighed. "They sent him to look into me, still suspicious of my going through with the abortion. I went no-contact with them from the day I left. They weren't allowed in my life as far as I was concerned. I went out of my way to hide Caleb from their ever finding out. I was scared they'd take him from me, and he was all I had left of you. Of our love." She wiped away the tears that fell.

"But he saw Caleb."

"Yeah." She nodded. "At first, I didn't know they sent him to find me. He met Caleb. But he didn't tell my parents. Wes became… infatuated with me. Obsessed with me. It was a sick, twisted mental warfare that he used on me. He saw me as a possession, and once I realized that he knew my parents, he used that link as a way to hold power over me. He threatened to tell them that I had a son if I didn't do as he said."

"To stay with him?" I asked, fearing that she'd lied about his abusing her. If he raped her and violated her, I'd never get over it.

"Yes. To keep me with him. It wasn't love. I knew that. I recognized that something had to be wrong with him, gravely wrong with him to act like this. When I started the job at the deli, I let Caleb go to stay with his friend, Brent. He met him through a pen pal program and they always stayed in touch. I knew that Brent's grandpa was a good guy, a war veteran, and I figured Caleb could stay there while I settled in during his spring break until I could know I found a decent sitter."

She rubbed her forehead. "That's why I had to live under the radar. To have a burner phone. To use cash. No trace and no record. My parents will go to the ends of the earth to ensure that no 'Mafia criminal blood' will be in their family."

"This is fucked up, Chloe. You understand this, right? This is fucked up."

"It is. But it's been my life, Franco. I've been running and hiding ever since the day I saw that positive line on that pregnancy test." She stood and rubbed her hands down her thighs. "I will never forsake him. I will never give him up. He is my son—"

"*Our* son. One I had a right to know about."

She shook her head. "Not if going to you would have put him at risk. Not if coming here would lead my parents to find him."

I paced faster, gripping my hair out of frustration.

"But how in the world did you find him?"

"Ethan is Liam's friend from the military," I answered, defeated and so twisted from her truth. "He noticed Wes lurking at his building."

She covered her mouth. "He was *still* looking for Caleb."

To bring him to your parents, who wished him dead from the beginning.

I couldn't speak. I could hardly wrap my head around it all. Words remained jumbled in my head, a mix of curses, raging complaints, and more demanding questions. I needed time, *a lot* more time, to process this bombshell that I was a father. All these years, I had a son and never knew.

"I am sorry, Franco." She set her hand over the base of her throat as she stared at me with tears in her eyes. "I am sorry, from the bottom of my heart. These last several days, I warred with the decision to tell you. I wanted to, so, *so* badly, but I feared the judgment you'd give me. I dreaded that you'd scowl at me like you are now. Like you hate me for deceiving you."

I licked my lips, feeling unsteady and on edge. I didn't know what I could tell her, what I would say. I was so mad, so hurt, and so stunned by all of this, I had no clue which way to go about my emotions.

"Can you find it in your heart to ever forgive me?" She asked it in such a small, nervous tone, something so uncharacteristic of her that it seemed like it wasn't even her. Vulnerable and afraid. She'd never been afraid of me. Not of my hurting her, and I almost wanted to laugh at the irony that not forgiving her would be punishment enough.

Numb and locked within the turbulent waves of anger and despair in my heart, I turned and walked away.

24

CHLOE

Franco walked away from me, shattering my heart and crushing my soul.

This was precisely why I didn't want to tell him. This was the reason I held back. I knew, I just *knew* he'd react poorly. I never once imagined a happy, gleeful moment when I told the man that I'd hidden his son from him for nine years. It simply wasn't positive news to break to anyone.

Yet, I wouldn't regret it. Running like I ran had kept Caleb alive. Hiding like I hid had ensured that my son stayed with me, healthy and normal, not controlled or killed by my parents.

I would never apologize for keeping my son a priority. I would never stop seeing to his safety.

But I wished from the bottom of my heart that I didn't have to hurt Franco in the process.

I wiped the remaining tears from my face and headed to the pool. Someone found a pair of swim trunks for Caleb, likely a pair from the housekeeper's son who sometimes took a dip when Olivia wanted someone to play with.

I stood at the edge of the room, smiling slightly at the cute scene.

Olivia splashed in her floatie while Caleb and Nicky, the head housekeeper's son, tossed a ball back to her.

Caleb was having the time of his life in the water and fooling around. He'd mentioned many times that he wanted a sibling. It was the first thing he wrote on every letter to Santa. It was the one item he asked for when he was tasked with writing a persuasive letter in school.

It felt good to see him enjoy others like this, and I wished against wishes that he could always have this kind of companionship.

"How are you doing?" Nina asked as she waddled from the pool. They'd made it a group affair, and I appreciated that they'd all teamed up to help distract Caleb while I spoke with Franco.

"I have no clue how to answer that," I said honestly.

She sat, sipping an icy glass of water, and tapped the chair next to her. "Sit. Talk. I know from experience that it is not good to bottle this stuff in."

"Ditto," Tessa said as she came close. We sat, and the chairs scraping over the tiles summoned Eva to draw near to our patio table too. Under the glass of the conservatory ceiling, we were warm and cozy with the sounds of the kids splashing under the watchful eyes of Dante and Romeo.

"Spill." Eva commanded it in that one-word instruction as Dante slipped out of the pool when Liam returned to it. The Mafia Boss took a chair at our table as well, holding Nina's hand, and I fought through the intimidation he caused me to feel.

"I didn't want to let anyone force me to have an abortion." I stared at Caleb, watching him play as I spoke quietly. I gave the women and Dante a condensed version of the story, and then I waited for *their* judgments too.

"I know I should've told Franco as soon as I saw him again." I shook my head.

"But with Wes going after you, and all the active danger…" Tessa sighed. "It was a lot at once."

"*If* Wes was the one who shot up that building," Dante argued. "We don't know if it was Wes who ordered that attack. While we can't trace those shooters to anyone else, it's a possibility, not a probability, that Wes ordered the shooters to target you."

Eva shook her head. "No. That doesn't make sense either. Why would he kill her? If he's so obsessed with her, he'd want her alive."

I frowned, thinking about what Caleb said, too. "If Wes knew that I was working at that deli, he would've been more likely to wait until I was done working and steal me away after a shift or something like that. But Caleb said that Wes was hanging out around him at Ethan's apartment."

"That doesn't mean Wes couldn't have hired men to shoot up your workplace," Nina argued. "He wouldn't have to be there to see that through."

"But why kill her at all?" Eva asked. "If his MO is to stalk her and try to own her, why hire men to potentially kill her?" She shook her head. "I bet he tracked Caleb, maybe not knowing where you were, and planned to use Caleb to make you run to him."

I shivered and rubbed my arms. It all sounded so terrible.

"*But,*" Tessa rushed to add, "none of that will matter anymore. You're here. You're safe. Both of you."

I swallowed hard and risked a direct look at Dante. He was watching me, serious and stern, but not mean.

"That's true. You're safe here," he said.

But what if I don't belong here? What if Franco can't ever get over this and wants me to leave after my lies and hiding his son?

I winced, entertaining a worse thought. *What if he tries to keep Caleb here where it's safe but get rid of me for how I broke his heart?*

After more platitudes and a little more conversation, Dante cleared his throat. "I'd like to speak with Chloe for a few minutes."

Oh, fuck.

Nina smiled at my expression. "You look like you were just summoned to the principal's office." She stood but leaned over to kiss his temple.

"Just to talk," he said as the women filed away.

Alone with the big, bad Mafia Boss, I waited for him to speak.

"Why?" he asked. "Why did you have to run when Franco could

have protected you?" He shook his head. "You met me. You met many of us. You knew that we took care of our own."

I nodded. "But my parents also knew how close I was to Franco and your family. If they were so determined to kill my son, they wouldn't have stopped just because I was under your family's protection."

He steepled his fingers on the wrought-iron table. "Are they coming to get you here now? You've been under our custody, a guest here, if you would, for a week now. Do you see them breaking in to find you?"

"They wouldn't need to find *me*. They'd need to find Caleb, and they almost succeeded. Wes was at the apartment building where Caleb was staying. I suspect Wes has gone rogue. He's on his own twisted mission to track me down or to find Caleb and use him to get me to go back to him. But if he still wants to bring me or Caleb back to my parents and is working for them, he almost reached him out there."

Just saying the words hurt. I couldn't fathom anything happening to my son.

"I was stuck. Then and now. If I came to Franco or anyone in your organization, it would've been another, easier way for them to find me. I have no doubt they would find out if I was here."

"But you have doubts that *I* couldn't keep my eyes on them?"

He had me there.

"Since you showed up here in the beginning of the week, I've had men on them. Watching them. Surveillance and tracing their calls."

I dropped my jaw. "You have?"

He nodded. "Want to know why?"

I swallowed hard.

"Because Franco is like my son. I treat him the same as I do Romeo. Even Liam. I don't let many people in my circle, but the ones I do, I look out for them." He sat up, straightening from his casual slouch. "Franco was devastated when you left. He was preparing an apartment for you two to start a new life. He was excited to provide for you, to see you go to college. Just as long as you stayed in his life and loved him, so he could love you. It's not often that people meet their soulmates so young in life, but I always assumed that was the case between you and Franco. He was never the same, Chloe. He mourned you. He missed you all that time, and the second he saw you again, it was like coming home. He *still* loves you, and I didn't want to risk your breaking him all over again. That's why I looked into your parents."

I cringed.

"Because I will not let you hurt him again."

I hung my head and exhaled a long and harsh breath. "I already have. By hiding his son from him."

"Tell me this. If you were so stuck when you were pregnant..." He tilted his head to the side, pensive. "I'll permit you that. You were scared, defensive of your baby. I praise you for running and hiding the way you did. *At first*. But what kept you from coming to Franco and telling him later? At any time in the last ten years?" He shook his head. "No. I can't understand why you didn't just come to my front door and tell me so I could reach him at that training."

"Because I didn't know if he would want to be bogged down with a baby. Our plans were to stay together while he trained. I'd go to college while he started his career for you as a soldier. He already had his mind set on becoming a capo one day. Think back to what he was like back then, Dante. Yes, we loved each other, but I also recognized how eager he was to start his job, to train and be the best soldier he could be for your family. I was nervous that he wouldn't want to start a family so young, and I didn't want to be an obstacle in the way of his commitment and duty to the job he was so excited to embrace."

He smirked and shook his head. "That argument won't work, Chloe. He was dedicated to his job. Yes, he was eager to prove himself and rise in the ranks. And he did. But a Constella soldier is not just an employee duty-bound to serve and protect us. They are part of the family. A member of a *family* here."

I lowered my gaze to the table. "I can see that."

"Do you? Do you understand it and see it now since you've been here?" He gestured at the people in this room. "We are a family. We're not mindless murderers like your parents are biased to assume we are. You can see now that this is a family that looks out for their own, right? We're not all terrible people."

I sighed and shook my head. "No. You're right. I do see it."

"We fight the good fight too, you know."

"I can tell." Why else would they go after Wes like that?

"And since Franco declared you—then and now—to be the woman he loves, that includes you. And your son."

"I appreciate it, Dante."

He nodded and glanced at Nina stepping into the pool. "We love each other and take care of each other because we're family."

"I know." It took me too long to realize it, but I was aware of how the Constella Family operated. "And now," I admitted on a sigh, "I need to find out if Franco can find it in his heart to forgive me."

He raised his brows. "Talk to him," he advised. "Don't assume a single thing and talk to him."

"I will." Just as soon as he would be willing to face me and hear me out again.

He stood. "I can't blame you for protecting Caleb. You were vulnerable and threatened, and I think, given the circumstances, you chose wisely until he was born. However, I wish you could have known that we'd always accept you and Caleb, and we'd always watch out for you. A love like what you and Franco have is not a fickle affair. It's the forever kind of love."

"I hope."

He paused before stepping away. "I think the term you'll be looking for is *grovel*, Chloe. Prepare to grovel."

I sighed, knowing this Mafia Boss was one hundred percent correct in that assessment.

25

FRANCO

For the rest of the day and evening, I holed myself up in the gym or my room. I knew Chloe wanted to speak to me. With the way I walked away from her, I was well aware that she wanted an answer to her question.

Could I forgive her? Of course, but I had to come to terms with all the lost time. All the heartache of missing out in such a huge way.

I'd never be able to reclaim the years I missed in Caleb's life. I would never have a chance to see any of his firsts and let him know that I cared.

I was torn with so many questions, curious about what that kid thought of me. He knew that I was his dad. He said he saw pictures of me. So he was allowed the courtesy of knowing about me, but I was in the dark about him.

It stung.

It ached.

My heart beat with pangs of sorrow and guilt, even though she was the one who'd kept him from me.

I couldn't sweat it out. I couldn't pace away from the mess in my head and heart. All day and night, I avoided everyone else and tried my best to get my mind clear enough to react logically.

Late at night, I gave up on trying to sleep and headed to the kitchen for water. When I reached the big room, I found Caleb sitting at the counter, peering around the room.

"Hey," I said quietly, not wanting to startle him. "Can't sleep?"

He yawned, a nonverbal argument to that idea. "I'm just thirsty. But I don't know where the cups are."

I got one for him and filled it with water.

"Thank you."

I took a seat across from him, marveling at how similar he was. He really was a mini me. The hair, the eyes, the spunk. But I saw Chloe in him too. I sighed, swallowing down the heartache of not being able to have watched him grow up. I'd missed out on too damn much.

I watched him drink the water, impressed that he didn't flinch. He stared right back at me, seeming as curious of me as I was of him.

I had no clue where to start. It was a late start, but I so badly wanted to get to know him.

I had no inclination to guess whether Chloe wanted me in his life at all. Hiding him from me since his conception was a pretty damn clear example of her choosing to shut me out.

"Have you known about me all your life? That I was your dad?" It seemed like a neutral question.

He shook his head. "No. Only when I was older."

I frowned, disliking the thought that came to mind. Did he ever think Wes was his dad?

"My mom told me about you when I was older and asked who my dad was. She had pictures and all, so I could see that you were a real person." He furrowed his brow. "You're a lot taller than I thought you'd be."

I chuckled.

He tipped his head to the side, eyeing me closely.

"What else doesn't match the pictures she had?"

"No, the pictures match. I'm just wondering if you'll keep her safe."

"Safe?"

He nodded. "I asked her why she didn't live with you and she said she wouldn't be safe. But now that she's by you, will you? Will you keep her safe?"

"Of course." I sighed. "No matter what, Caleb, I will always do everything in my power to keep both you and her safe."

"Can you beat up Wes for bothering her?" he asked.

I grunted a laugh. "You want me to beat him up?"

He nodded, stern and serious. "My mom reminds me that violence isn't the answer in most cases. But I think Wes really needs a good ass kicking for being so mean and weird to her."

I smirked. "Does your mom think you should be saying something like ass kicking?"

He shook his head. "I won't tell if you don't."

"Nah, not like that." I shook my head. "Don't start a habit of lying to her."

He hung his head. "I know. And I'm just joking. But I really wish she didn't have to worry about Wes. He's so creepy. I hate him."

"Just remember what I said. I will always do everything in my power to keep you and your mom safe." I refused to go into detail. I couldn't. But this boy—my boy—could rest assured that Wes wouldn't be bothering anyone once I got ahold of him.

"Thanks. You're a good guy, Mr. Franco." He stood and nodded, acting wiser than his age. "I got a good vibe about you."

Nine-year-olds can sense vibes? I crossed my arms and smiled as he set the glass in the sink. "Yeah? A good vibe?"

"Yeah. You're a cool dude." He yawned again. "Goodnight."

"Goodnight." I held my breath, watching him go. Once he was out of sight, I let out a heavy sigh. It didn't cover the sound of a sniffle.

I turned to catch Chloe standing at the other end of the room, leaning against the doorway. She probably watched and heard that whole conversation.

I stared at her, wishing this didn't have to be so hard between us. As she sniffled again and wiped away her tears, she cleared her throat. "I—"

She cut herself off, turning and rushing away.

"No," I growled quietly as I rushed to my feet.

I'd had it with this.

I was sick of her running.

She belonged with me.

I caught up to her in the hallway that led to the guest room she'd been sleeping in. Grabbing hold of her wrist, I held on to her and tugged her to follow me. With a heated look, a worried glance that spoke volumes, she met my gaze and came with me to my room.

I closed and locked the door, stalking after her as she backed up.

"Why did you run?" I asked.

She tipped her chin up. "Because I don't want to hurt you anymore."

"Then don't."

She furrowed her brow as I reached for the belt of her robe.

"Stay," I told her as I shoved at her robe, urging the material to fall to the carpet.

"Will you forgive me?"

I put my hand on her side and tugged her close. "Only if you stay." I crushed my lips against her mouth, unable to help myself. I couldn't help myself when she was near.

"I will stay as long as you let me," she vowed.

"I will always forgive you," I said as I bunched her nightgown and pulled it up over her head to remove it, "as long as you understand that I fucking love you."

She gasped as I kissed her hard, walking her toward the bed.

"I love you, Chloe, and I will never stand for anyone to hurt you. You or our son."

She nodded, reaching for my shirt to pull it up.

"I have spent too many years missing you."

"I hated every second of them." She shoved at my pants next.

"I don't ever want to lose you again."

She tripped over her panties as she shoved them off. With every step we took in this rushed, fumbling dance, we kissed and stripped.

I pushed her to the bed, feasting my eyes on the sight of my one true love lying there for me.

"Tell me right now, Chloe, if I'm good enough for you to stay. If I'm worthy of your love."

She nodded, staring me in the eye and bewitching me. "I have never stopped loving you. Even when I ran." She slid her legs wider apart. "I love you, and you have always been worthy of my love."

I got it now. I saw in the depth of her soulful gaze that she believed it. That she meant it. But she also had a big enough heart and a smart, level head to know that running when she was pregnant was the best way to make sure he lived. That our son survived. That our love would carry on in him.

"Can you forgive me?" she asked, begging in a shy, hopeful tone.

I knelt down, then hovered over her. As I kissed her hard, bracing my weight on my forearm, I angled my dick to her and lined up to drive home.

"Yes, Chloe." I slammed all the way into her tight, wet heat. "I forgive you." I pulled out and pushed in fully once more. "I love you." Again, I tortured her tight pussy. "And I will never, ever give up on you."

She moaned, arching up into me to match me thrust for thrust. "And I will never give up on us."

"No matter what," I growled between kisses as I slammed into her faster and faster.

"No matter…" She gasped, already so close to coming. "No matter what."

I kissed her, stealing her breath and muffling her loud cries as she came. Squeezing me tight, she wrapped her legs around my waist and clung to me as though she couldn't bear a single inch of a gap between us.

"I love you," I told her as she caught her breath from her first orgasm. Tonight called for a celebration. Of no more lies. Of coming together, of promising not to let anything stand in the way of our future again.

"I love you so much," she replied, breathing raggedly.

I pulled out and turned her onto her hands and knees, taking her from behind as I chased my release, determined to fuck this logic into her.

She and I belonged together. For good. And I spent all night proving how right it felt to surrender to each other.

26

CHLOE

I lost track of the orgasms Franco gave me. Over and over, he pounded into me. As soon as we came and cleaned up, he'd start again. With our hands and mouths, we revved each other up in foreplay. He knew what I liked, and I remembered what he enjoyed.

That was the beauty of reuniting with a former love.

Not former. Current. And forever love. I hope.

It didn't help that we shared all these lasting vows and sentiments in the heat of the moment. With the haze of lust and the deep addiction of desire ruling us as we came together again and again all night long, we weren't thinking or speaking clearly. At least I wasn't. He had me so sated and needy, back and forth, that I barely knew my name.

At last, when we both seemed ready to pass out for the rest of the night, we lay on our sides. Facing each other and staring into each other's familiar eyes, we let the mood shift. Gone was the frantic hunger to fuck the night away. Now was the time to calm down and talk.

"Was he an easy baby?" he asked.

I loved that he wanted to know it all.

"Yes and no. His birth was."

He sighed, frowning. "But you didn't even have medical care. That was risky as hell, wasn't it? I see all the appointments and such that Nina goes through and it seems like a lot."

"I was fortunate with a very easy and simple pregnancy. I didn't have many symptoms. I seldom got sick. I worried that the stress of running away would harm him, but it didn't. He was an easy delivery and a perfectly healthy baby. My friends who were in the vet program were angels in disguise, and I'll never forget that they helped me hide Caleb's birth."

He scowled. "So he doesn't have a birth certificate?"

"He does, but..." I winced, hating that I did this. "I had it covered up with a fake one. I'm sure I can have it fixed one day and all."

He nodded. "We'll clear it up."

I smiled at him. I bet he wanted to be on the certificate and he'd pay to make it so.

"I just had to go to such extremes to make sure my parents couldn't find him. Or me. It was hard at first. Everything is digital and trackable. I haven't renewed my driver's license in years. No health insurance to file. Everything. It was eye opening. But I did my best for Caleb. I got prenatal vitamins. I went to health clinics for ultrasounds. It might have been risky going to a vet for delivery help, but it was sanitary, obviously. A roommate knew a doula, and hell, veterinarians deliver mammals and humans are mammals too."

He slanted his brows, skeptical about that.

"It was the best I could do. Hiding and keeping Caleb safe mattered the most. Sometimes, I worried that my parents would try to have me killed if I had him, and fear is a hell of a motivator to hide well."

"I hate that you went through this."

I sighed. "It wasn't easy, but I had to. I couldn't give up on our baby. It was a symbol of *our* love, and I would never let that die. I'd rather you think I left you and hate me than let our baby suffer. Caleb was made from our love, and that's something I'll always treasure and protect."

"He was a good baby, though?" he asked again.

"He was. He latched on well, but then it was hard to wean him off when I was exhausted from breastfeeding after he turned one. Like any baby, he had his difficult phases. I also looked for the older, grandmotherly kind of sitters to watch him. Never a daycare. Always paid them under the table and all."

He smiled. "He sure looks healthy and cared for."

"And he's a good boy. He's got your attitude sometimes, so tough and even cocky at times. He'll try to push me and test his limits, but he's got a good heart."

"I see that already. I haven't known him for a full day yet and I'm already proud of him."

I framed his face and leaned in close to kiss him once. "I'm proud of him too." I thought back to how Caleb didn't think twice about reaching out to prevent Olivia from getting hurt.

"Single moms are tough," he said. "My mom was mostly single since my dad passed away young."

And his mom died just before we started dating. He hadn't lacked for a family, though, working for Dante. He had Romeo, even Eva in the distance. I had both of my parents and lacked support and love.

"Caleb always knew he had a father, just that you weren't in the picture."

"Did he ask why?"

I nodded. "He asked more about grandparents at first. Why he didn't have two pairs of them. Why he didn't have any of them. That was about the time he asked about his dad, and I never lied. I always told him your name. I showed him the pictures I had of us."

He smiled slightly. "I like knowing I was… there. In his mind." Then he frowned. "But I hate the idea of his thinking I wanted nothing to do with him."

I shook my head. "I never let him have that impression. I was careful not to set it up for him to have bad ideas of you. I tried not to tell him too much, and I think he's so perceptive that he realized how it pained me to talk about you. He asked me many times if I missed you, and I did. I told him that I did. I think he stopped asking because he didn't want to see me sad."

"He didn't assume anyone else was his dad?" He brushed my hair back as he stared at me, calm and not mad.

"No. I dated a couple of guys, just one-night flings to see if I could get over you." I shook my head. "I couldn't. After a condom broke and I got pregnant and miscarried, I didn't want to even deal with another man again. I tried and failed to get my tubes tied, but I was too young."

"Fuck." He kissed my brow. "I'm so sorry to hear that."

I nodded. "And then when Wes came into our lives, I never let Caleb treat him as a replacement for a father. He wasn't a father figure to him. He never paid attention to him or tried to interact with him. Wes treated Caleb as a thing that was just there in the background. Caleb never tried to view Wes as a father figure."

"Good."

I smiled. "Caleb always knew your name. Whenever he drew family pictures, you were there. For a while, he misspelled your name as *Franko*."

He laughed a bit at that, but he sobered quickly.

"Ask me anything," I pleaded. "I enjoy this. I want you to know everything. I feel terrible about all that you've missed." Because it was so clear that he would've been such a good, involved, and hands-on dad. I almost felt foolish to think that I did a better job on my own now, but I stood by my conviction that I kept Caleb as safe as *I* could. That relying on only myself, trusting only my resources, I could ensure that he lived and thrived.

"Were you ever going to tell me?" he asked, softly and almost with that gut-wrenching hint of sorrow. "If you didn't happen to get a job at the A&J and work there that night when the shooting happened, would you have ever reached out to me and told me?"

"I wanted to." I gazed into his eyes, letting him see the truth behind my reply. "I wanted to tell you so many times. I dreamed of these best-case scenarios, these fantasies of whimsical Utopia. That I'd tell you and it would be a fairytale ending."

"But you didn't. Not once over all those years."

I shook my head as shame returned. "But I didn't know how I could. I had no way to know how you'd react. If you'd be mad and turn me away. I was nervous to come near home and be by any Constella member out of the fear that my parents would find me through you, knowing how close I was to you once. It was a link I feared they'd somehow exploit."

"I understand that, but…" He sighed and lowered his gaze.

"All those years, the last seven of them, I spent so much time and effort escaping Wes that I didn't have the freedom to plan a visit to talk to you. I feared sending an email. A text. A call. I was trapped, and all I could focus on was getting by. Just making life tolerable, staying afloat, and praying nothing ever happened to me or Caleb."

"But that's no way to live."

I nodded. "Not at all. It was simply a way to survive."

"Not anymore." He kissed my brow, and I smiled at his tenderness.

I dreamed of hearing those words so many times. I fell asleep imagining great scenes like this one, and now that the moment was here, that it was happening, I was tempted to pinch myself and know that I was awake and this was reality, my reality. After all the sadness and yearning for him, he was here and vowing to give me a real life. "Just surviving" wasn't an option with him.

"But what does that mean?"

He huffed. "Were you so lost to coming and not listening to a single word I said earlier?"

I frowned playfully. "Oh, like you didn't go a little crazy back there?"

"You make me crazy." He kissed me softly. "In the best of ways."

"I recall your mumbling some incoherent nonsense when you came the first time."

His answering smile was slow and sure. I was glad that this part of him never changed, his smugness that he only revealed when he was being goofy and playful with me.

"That's how you know you're doing it right. When you can't talk, much less think."

I nestled into the pillow, determined to be serious again. "What did you mean, though?"

"About what?"

"About how we could be together. How this would work." I shrugged. "How Caleb would fit into your life."

"We stay together."

I raised my brows. "Just like that? Here?"

"I have a house next door. Eva and Liam do too. Tessa and Romeo are a little further out with this renovation project that never seems to be finished. I think they just like staying here too much."

I scrunched my face. "It doesn't get crowded?"

He snorted a laugh. "You have seen how huge this place is, right?"

"I mean..." I smirked, but it turned into a grin. "Dante and Romeo, you know. Dad and son. Then Nina and Tessa are BFFs. So with the age gaps and all... I'm guessing Nina is younger than Romeo by a bit?"

He chuckled. "It's a little complex. But you're not suggesting there's a reason to worry about incest, are you?"

I laughed louder, loving how easy it could be to joke with him, to laugh with him. We used to be like this all the time. I was kicking myself for how long I fought telling him. Had I cleared the air sooner, we could've enjoyed this whole week.

No. I'm not doing that. I refused to call myself stupid for hesitating. Owning up to my secret took guts, and I wasn't a fool to be nervous. With all that I'd suffered and survived, I stood by my right to be guarded when it came to Caleb.

But of course, Franco would want to protect Caleb too. Now that I'd lived here and witnessed how ruthless these men were, I *knew* they'd keep my life secure. Against Wes. Against my parents. Franco had my back.

"No, I'm not suggesting anything like incest." I rolled my eyes.

"I know. I know. I'm just teasing. But seriously, there is plenty of room for all of us. My place doesn't have that indoor pool room in the conservatory, but we're all in and out of here every day, anyway."

I grew giddy, excited about my future. "So, just like that, you're saying I should move in with you?"

He furrowed his brow. "No."

My expression fell.

"I'm saying you should marry me."

27

FRANCO

For the rest of my life, I would cling to this memory. Stunning Chloe silent. Wowing her and maybe giving her a little dose of actual shock.

Her mouth dropped after I told her my intentions. Her lips remained parted in an O that gave me filthy ideas. It was nice to know my girl still loved giving head. But it was even nicer to know that she wanted to stay with me.

For good, I hoped. Officially, as my wife.

We were only ten years late to make it happen.

"Will you marry me, Chloe Dawson?"

She clamped her lips shut and strained to swallow. Not long ago, before we started talking and relaxing, she seemed sleepy and lazy, so lax snuggled in bed with me. Now, her eyes were wide open. Clear and alert.

"What did you just say?"

I grinned, enjoying this way, way too much. I'd wanted to say those words to her so many times when we were younger. We talked about marriage and loosely agreed that, yeah, of course, we'd get married one day. We were adamant back then that we were soulmates, that it was Kismet for us to meet and fall in love, no matter how young we were. According to that one saying, *When you know, you know.* Well, when we knew, we knew.

"Marry me, Chloe." I slid closer to her, needing to feel more of her soft, warm body flush to mine. "I won't let you go again. I hated that I did before. I won't let you go. Or Caleb. I want you both in my life for good, officially."

"Oh, Franco…" She sighed, speechless for more. Her eyes shone with tears, but the happy smile on her face led me to believe she was holding back tears of joy.

"I want a chance to get to know my son. *Our* son. I want a chance to have another child with you. All the kids we want. I've lost too much time with you, and I want the opportunity to have my time now."

She sniffled, blinking back the tears that built along her lids. "I'm… Damn. Sorry. You're overwhelming me."

"In a good way?"

She leaned in to kiss me. "In a very good way! This is more than I ever could have counted on happening."

"Why?" I had to understand. "What will it take to show you that I love you with all that I am?"

Her smile was soft and delicate. "I feared you'd be so mad. All this time, the longer I kept Caleb from you, my fears worsened and deepened. I was nervous to get my hopes up too high. This is, literally, all that I could have ever dreamed for."

I wiped my thumbs over her cheeks, swiping the stubborn tears away. "Don't cry."

"It's a happy cry." She kissed me again. "I dared to hope that you'd still love me. I'm not doubting you. I'm battling the walls I built up to protect myself. I'm knocking over all the times I told myself to be realistic, the assumptions that I stacked up that claimed you'd never forgive me for hiding your son from you."

"If you'd tried to hide him for any other reason than to keep him safe…"

She shook her head. "No. Hell no. He's your son, and I wanted you to have each other. It was all the other stuff in life that stood in the way. You don't understand how hard it was. I ran from you. I broke it off with you in such a bold, sudden, and harsh manner by taking off without a goodbye. Yet, you loved me enough and knew yourself enough not to pursue me."

"It was hard. So many times, I talked myself into looking for you, but I refrained from messing it up. I figured that you made your answer clear, that you didn't want me."

"No, Franco. Not at all. And in your not fighting for me, not chasing me, I was 'free' to experience the opposite. When I broke it off with Wes after only a few months, he couldn't let me go. He was deranged. Obsessed. And in that difference, I saw how stupid I was to ever let you go."

"You're stuck with me now."

She nodded, seeming excited to cling to that promise.

"But I need to know if *you* can be stuck with me."

Her face changed to a deep frown as she reared back to look at me fully. "What do you mean?"

"Can you adjust to living with me? Living here and knowing what the family does?"

She'd always known. We started and built our relationship when she was a senior in high school, aware that the Constella name represented the Mafia. Her parents did their best to taint her views of what such an organization was like. That if it was a *crime* family, every member was automatically evil to the bone and the default enemy of anyone on the right side of law.

That was erroneous in so many ways, but most of all in the manner that grayness was unaccounted for. Supposedly, good people like cops, such as Wes Morrison, could do very bad things like abusing power and stalking defenseless women. Whereas, reputedly bad people like us Mafia men could do heroic things like killing true sinners and saving those who needed security.

"Can you try to adjust to this sort of life? Where sometimes the danger is higher and we need to lock down in the houses? When you'll need to have bodyguards around you and Caleb at times?"

She sucked on her lower lip.

"It's not always a world of high stakes like it is right now. It's not always a constant of danger right on our doorstep. We do all we can to keep our homes as safe and free of business as possible."

"I can see that," she replied. "Nina, Tessa, and Eva have tried to explain a lot of this."

I was glad that she had them. And that they had her. All four of them clicked like sisters.

"Most of the danger at the moment will be over soon."

"With... the Giovannis?" she guessed.

"Yes. Dante, Romeo, and I, Liam as well, we're very confident that our two top enemies will cancel each other out. The Devil's Brothers MC and the Giovanni Family. We've been monitoring them and investigating both groups. It's been a waiting game, because if we were to attack both, we'd be outnumbered. But any day now, we'll get the news that they'd eliminated each other as they're equally prone to infighting and making stupid, rash decisions that get people killed."

Her sigh was soft against my face, and I was glad that she didn't break eye contact. I knew this was hard for her. She was soft and light and all things that were good. I would always keep my darkness from her, but I had to know if she could compromise.

"What about Wes?"

I frowned. "What about him? I'll kill him." Coming out with that fact as bluntly as possible was the best method to discuss it. To the point and honest. Wes Morrison would be dead for all he'd done.

"Even if he wasn't the one who put the hit out for those men to shoot the deli?"

"Of course. I will not let that man be a threat to the woman I love."

To her credit, she didn't flinch. Here I was telling her, point blank, that I intended to murder a man, and she didn't blink or wince.

"I wished so many times that he'd die." Her admission was a weak, carefully given whisper, and that surprised me even more. It was proof that she could lean between the black-and-white rigidity of good versus evil.

"So many times," she repeated, firming her expression into one of pain and anger. "He was a monster to stalk me, to try to con me and trap me."

"And we don't need monsters like that in the world."

She nodded. "So long as I remember that, that some monsters will get what they deserve, it's nothing more than a reminder that Karma is at work."

I exhaled a breath of relief. I wanted her to keep her goodness, her innocence, but it soothed me to know she was flexible with her moral compass, too. The last thing I needed was for her to assume I was a perfect hero who did no wrong. I never wanted her to view me as a villain, not completely.

"What's your answer, Chloe?" I was determined to steer this conversation back on track. "Will you marry me?"

She nodded. "Yes, Franco, I'll—"

I frowned. Watching my reaction, she went still.

"Wait. Never mind."

She gaped at me. "What?"

"Before you officially accept, I need to ask Caleb for his permission to marry you."

She swooned, actually cooing an *aww* that made me smile.

I didn't miss how protective he was of her. First when he asked if I'd keep her safe. Then further back, when he said he didn't care if Wes was bothering him because it meant that Chloe was spared.

I didn't want to barge into their family unit. All his life, that boy knew her as his mother in real time and only my name and likeness in a photo.

I wanted to do this right, and asking Caleb for his permission would go a long way toward understanding where our priorities should be.

"I love you, Franco."

I kissed her. "I love you too."

Finally, after years of trying to get over her and failing, I knew why.

It was impossible. We belonged together. As we lay together and closed our eyes, we fell asleep with the idea that tomorrow would bring us one day closer to the happy ending we should've had years ago.

28

CHLOE

Something I considered a mom clock ticked on. I woke up well before Franco did, attuned to the intrinsic need to make breakfast for my boy.

I didn't know how I did it. It just worked. My body was programmed to always take care of him, and somehow, I woke up when I knew he'd be ready to rise. Maybe it was a biological phenomenon. Maybe it was crap and I was imagining things, but I liked to think that I was simply attuned to where my son was and what he might need.

In the kitchen, I joined Dante and Eva as they argued over the best way to make eggs.

"For fuck's sake, Uncle Dante," Eva declared. "The baby isn't going to know the difference between Nina eating fried eggs or scrambled eggs!"

I bit my lip to stifle a laugh.

"Am I right?" Eva held out the spatula at me.

Dante narrowed his eyes at me, and I was surprised by how domestic it was. Never mind the fact that these people afforded a hefty household staff. They were in here like ordinary people, preparing food themselves.

"Uh…" I shrugged. "Eggs are eggs."

Dante rolled his eyes. "Well, Nina hardly touched breakfast all week when I made them scrambled. I think she might prefer fried."

"And I think you, my dear uncle, are so thoroughly pussy-wh—"

I lunged forward to cover her mouth with my hand. "Good morning!" I said cheerily to Caleb as he entered the room.

He eyed us carefully, then shook his head. "If you're worried about me hearing a bad word, Nicky said I'd learn them all in a day."

Dante shrugged. "We try."

I let Eva go. "Ha!" She barked out one wry laugh. "We barely try. Liv's in her parrot phase and repeating everything that resembles a naughty word."

"Dante," I said. "If Nina is picky about her breakfasts, it might be because she can't eat as much."

He frowned, and it endeared him to me that much more. This Mafia Boss, so worried about his pregnant wife's appetite. It was oddly sweet from someone who should be so gruff.

"There's not a lot of room for food anymore," I advised.

"I suppose," he said.

Nina entered the kitchen then, the same as the head housekeeper and Nicky. He hurried to sit with Caleb, fitting right in despite the employment barrier his mom had.

"I'll tell you," Nina said with a wince. "There's not a lot of room for this baby anymore, either." She put her hand on her back as she sat on a high stool.

Dante dropped the spatula and hurried to her side. "Are you okay?"

"I think the baby is coming today."

Dante shared a look with Eva. "But Danicia isn't here. She's on vacation this week."

"Then you have to take me to the hospital and someone else can help me have this baby!"

I patted Caleb's head as I walked past him. "Cereal or eggs?" I asked him.

Nicky slid a box of cereal over. "Want these?"

Caleb nodded, taking a bowl from the stack. He glanced at Nina and looked at me. "Is she *really* having a baby today? Here?"

I shrugged. *Doubt it.*

"How are you feeling?" I asked Nina.

She grimaced but morphed the expression into something of a surprised smile. "Hey! You know how this feels. Help."

I laughed. "What do you feel?"

"Like I'm having a baby."

I nodded. "All right... Did your water break?"

She shook her head, then frowned and looked at Dante. "Did I?"

He shook his head as well. "No...? The bed was dry."

I cleared my throat and sat next to Nina. "It's early yet."

"That's why I'm freaking out!"

"Have you started feeling Braxton-Hicks yet?" I laid my hand on her arm and rubbed softly. If she was having her baby, comforting touches might help. It did for me, but no two women were the same.

She gripped my hand, ceasing movement.

Okay. She's not a touchy-feely type.

"I don't know!" she wailed. "I can't tell what they feel like, if I've felt them, or how they should feel. When Danicia and my other doctor explain them, it sounds like nothing I can understand."

"Okay. Okay. So they feel like real contractions—"

"That doesn't help."

"But they don't increase and last as long as the real ones do." I smiled, hoping to reassure her. "When it's time for the baby to come, you'll know."

She narrowed her eyes. "How?"

I shrugged and winced a bit. "I don't know. Honestly, I think it's just a saying people tell you to throw you off."

She groaned.

"There you are," Dante said as Romeo came into the room.

"What's wrong with her?" he asked of Nina.

"I'm pregnant, that's what." She cringed. "That's not what I mean. I'm glad to be pregnant. I'm excited. But I'm *this* pregnant and I can't tell if I'm having the baby."

Romeo's eyes bugged out. "Now?"

"Okay, okay. Let's take this down a notch. Nina? Are you having anything that resembles a contraction anywhere right now?"

She pursed her lips and uttered a quiet, sheepish, "No."

"Then we'll watch it," I advised.

"Are you sure?" Dante asked. He had his phone in his hand, seeming ready to call for help.

"Well, I'm not a doctor, but I was pregnant before." I patted Nina's arm and she latched on to it, gripping my hand like it was a lifeline.

"I'm so happy you're here."

She said it because I was uniquely able to sympathize with what she was experiencing, but her words touched me, anyway.

"I'm happy to be here." As Franco entered the kitchen and caught my eye, I smiled. "And I'm happy to stay here."

"Oh, shit." Franco looked at Nina's distressed expression. "Are you having the baby now?"

"I think you're supposed to say *oh shoot*," Caleb said. "So the young ones don't hear bad words."

"Whoops." Franco nodded at him.

"Why *can't* I have the baby today?" she snapped at him.

"For one thing, it's too early," I reminded her.

"Because I need to chat with Caleb first," he replied.

My heart beat faster, knowing why they'd have a conversation.

"And we need to discuss what happened last night," Romeo said, looking at Dante.

"What happened last night?" I asked. *Wes? Did someone find him and kill him?* I didn't feel bad about wishing for it.

"The 'war' is done," Dante answered.

Franco nodded. "Reports came in overnight that the Devil's Brothers MC and the Giovannis eliminated each other."

I appreciated that he toned down his announcement around Caleb. It would take some adjusting to inform him about what this family represented.

"So." Franco pointed at Nina. "Baby emergency or no?"

Nina looked at me expectantly.

I laughed lightly. "Maybe not yet."

"Okay. Caleb, wanna see the basketball court?" Franco said.

"Yeah!" Caleb wiped his face off with a napkin and hurried off his stool.

"Aw, shoot." Nicky sighed. "I gotta get to school. I'll see you later."

Caleb nodded. "Okay." Then he stopped rushing and backtracked for his cereal bowl, grabbed it, emptied the milk in the sink, and set it in there.

"This way," Franco said, leading him toward the sliding glass doors to the side.

Eva and Nina stared at the sink. Dante and Romeo did as well.

"You did a good job raising that boy," Dante said.

I smiled. "I know. But Franco will help too."

Dante nodded, seeming happy about that. "If you need me," he told Nina, "*at all*, I'll be in my office talking with Romeo. Okay?"

She waved him off, nodding. "Okay."

Dante glanced at me and I gave him a thumbs-up.

"Oh, damn," Eva said. "I need to get Liv up before her checkup." With one more glance at me, then Nina, she hesitated. "Everything good here?"

"Yeah," I replied.

"I'll let everyone know if today's the day," Nina said.

Once we were alone, I snacked on the toast that was set out and grabbed a coffee. "Feeling anything?"

"Dumb."

I smirked at her.

"I do! I've never done this before."

"Fair enough, but trust me, you'll realize something is up."

"Did you?"

I nodded. "I suddenly stood in a puddle and felt like I had to poop. Badly."

"That's not very descriptive. The second part."

"You don't often stand in a puddle that gushed out of you, right?"

She shook her head. "I suppose that part is obvious. It's just so scary. The unknown. How the hell did you cope on your own?"

"The same as you. Clueless and worried I was dumb." I smiled. "I think every woman feels like that."

"First-time moms, at least."

I glanced again in the direction of the sliding glass doors, wondering how Caleb and Franco were faring out there.

"Everything okay?" she asked me, noticing where I was looking.

I laughed. "Shouldn't I be the one asking you that?"

"Distract me. What's going on with you and Franco? That was a hell of a bombshell you dropped yesterday."

I nodded. "We talked last night. And… then some."

She grinned. "Sounds promising so far. Just seeing you two smiling like that is a good sign. And his wanting to talk to Caleb."

I nodded and leaned in. "Can you keep a secret?"

"Ooh. You're really rocking it in the keeping-the-pregnant-lady-distracted department. Yes, I want to hear a secret."

"I asked if you could keep one?"

"For how long?" She arched a brow.

"Not long." I glanced again at the doors, wondering what was said so far. I wondered if Franco had a ring already.

She gestured for me to spill.

"Franco wants to ask Caleb for permission to marry me."

She slapped her hand over her mouth but a loud gasp came out loudly before she covered it.

"What?" Dante rushed out of his office, where he must have kept the door open. "What? What is it?"

"Girl talk," she sassed, waving at him to shoo him away.

Facing me, she exaggerated a grin. "He does? Is that what he's doing right now?"

"I think so." I nodded. "He wants to be a father to Caleb."

"Ooh, this is so—*fuck!*" She winced and laid her hand on her stomach.

Dante ran back out. "Nina?"

But her wince was gone. "False alarm."

Romeo slowed after his father, sighing.

Once they left again, she smiled at me. "This is so exciting. I'm so thrilled for you. This is wonderful news! When I first met Franco, I thought he was so subdued. Quiet. I always wondered what his story was, assuming he had been heartbroken before. Getting to see him around you solves it all. He's your soulmate. It's just so obvious. And I'm so happy for you both that you've found your way back to each other."

I leaned my head on her shoulder. "Thanks, Nina."

"I can't wait to see our family grow. More to enjoy."

I couldn't wait either. The idea of finally having my dreams come true felt so surreal. "But... maybe tell his little girl or boy to sit tight for a couple more weeks."

"It is too early," she worried.

"Not *too* early, but the longer they stay in, the better."

"Was Caleb on time?"

I laughed. "He was five days past my due date."

"Oh, wow. I'm so impatient to meet our little one now."

"Hang in there," I advised. Looking out the sliding glass doors again, I tried to coach myself to do the same.

I was nervous but excited. Everything was changing so fast, but I respected that Franco would go at Caleb's pace. If he was ready for us to marry, great. If he needed a little more time to get used to the idea of it, then we'd wait. Franco's consideration of Caleb's opinions and reactions was so sweet, so touching that I had more than enough proof that he was going to be an excellent father to our son.

Hang in there. Be patient. Just a little longer and I'll have my answer about whether I'll finally be able to become Mrs. Franco Constella.

29

FRANCO

"This is so cool!" Caleb was in awe of everything I showed him. The gym, the huge yard, the outdoor pool that wasn't open yet, the tennis courts no one really used. Even though this wasn't my main residence, I wouldn't be opposed to living here for good.

I had a hunch that Chloe would like staying by Nina and the other women. Based on how Nina leaned on Chloe just now, it seemed that their friendship was mutual.

If staying in the big house made it easier for Caleb to adjust, fine by me. I wanted to spoil them both. I intended to let them tell me what they wanted or needed and I would make it happen.

How could I not?

I was over the moon, so grateful that I had them in my life. It seemed natural to bend over backward and treat them like the treasures they were.

By the time we got to the basketball court, he seemed at ease with me showing him around.

"Can I play with Nicky?" he asked.

"Now?" Damn, I was hoping to talk with him a bit.

"Whenever." He shrugged before grabbing a basketball from the rack and bouncing it. "When Mom and I visit here."

I smiled. "What if you lived here?"

His jaw dropped. "Seriously?"

I clapped for him to pass me the ball. Dante was the swimmer. Romeo liked to run. But I enjoyed all sports and forms of fitness. Caleb passed the ball to me, and we started a little back and forth.

"What would you think about living here?" I asked.

"As long as Mom is safe, cool."

This boy. He loved his mother, and I was so damn proud of him for putting her first. She put him first, though. And I would too.

"This house is extremely safe," I said. It was. Since the bikers tried to break in and take Olivia for leverage, we ramped up the home security. Dante was already on it, requesting the tightest patrolling efforts with Nina here and expecting their baby.

"I saw the guards when we came."

I nodded.

"And the fences. And the gates. And the guys who looked like SWAT men."

I smiled. "Yep. All of them secure this home."

"How come?"

"We run an organization that specializes in many things, and we've been successful."

"You mean you're rich," he clarified.

"Very wealthy," I replied carefully, without a note of bragging. "And sometimes, other people want to take our success and power—"

"And money?" he guessed.

"Yes, and that's where the security measures come into play."

For the next fifteen minutes, he peppered me with tons of questions. Could he pick his room. Would he be able to go to school with Nicky. Was the pool inside always open. How would he be able to go to the library.

On and on, he asked me countless questions. I remained patient, answering all of them. It couldn't be easy for him to adjust to a new home when Chloe had just relocated them from Philadelphia to run from Wes.

With every question, he showed me a little more about what he was interested in or curious about. He sought stability and the freedom to do things as he pleased, and that was justified.

All throughout his interrogation, we played some light ball. Mostly passing the ball back and forth, but also seeing if we could drive the ball past each other. I gave him the tip that if he ever played out here against Dante or Romeo, they'd understand a tug on his left ear meant he intended to feint to the right.

Eventually, he moved on to the harder questions. "What are your intentions with my mom?"

I bit back a laugh at his wording. So formal. And direct.

"Would it be all right with you if I married her?"

He stopped dribbling and stared at me, the ball at his hip.

"You..." He frowned. "You want my permission?"

I nodded. "Yeah. She's your mom and I know you care about her. You've been looking out for her for a long while, and I'd like to help with that."

He lowered his gaze, blinking. "You want to marry my mom?"

"We dated a long time ago and fell in love."

"And still love each other now." He lifted his chin. "I can tell. She was always so sad when she said she missed you."

This boy didn't even know me but he saw that.

"I missed her too."

"What made you break up?" he asked.

I didn't want to scare him or paint Chloe in a bad light. "Some people tried to get between us."

He nodded, seeming so pensive.

"What would you think if I married her?" I asked again.

"Yeah." He nodded quickly. "That would be all right."

I smiled at him, knowing I would have the time of my life learning how to be this boy's father.

Before I could say anything, he ran at me. The ball dropped and rolled away as he darted toward me. He wrapped his arms around me and caught me in a tight hug.

My heart fucking melted. My son was here, hugging me. I'd cherish this moment forever. He was trying to act so cool and mature, so indifferent like nothing could faze him, but he was so young and impressionable. And not too old or cool to want to hug me.

"I'm glad you're my dad."

I hugged him back the best I could at this angle. "And I'm glad you're my son."

Goddammit. Tears stung at my eyes, and I breathed in deeply to keep them at bay. This was one of the happiest moments of my entire life.

Nothing could go wrong. I felt stronger, better, more whole, just in knowing this boy would teach me how to be the best dad ever.

"Franco!"

I tensed. My heart raced as my instinct to fight kicked in. Adrenaline rushed through me.

"Franco!"

I gripped Caleb and forced him behind me, shielding him at Chloe's frantic yell. Then I turned toward the house, reaching for the gun in my holster, hidden under my jacket.

She ran out the sliding doors. Her eyes were wide as she inhaled to yell again. "Hurry! Her water broke. The baby is coming today!"

"Whoa!" Caleb said behind me.

I fought back the fear that choked me at her yell. That was how quickly I developed the instinct to protect our son. As I came to terms with the fact that no one was attacking and nothing worse had happened to warrant her loud shout of alarm, I exhaled in relief.

"Scratch that," Chloe said as Nina groaned from further inside. "The baby is coming right now!"

30

CHLOE

"I told you I don't know what I'm doing!" Nina wailed.

I wasn't alarmed by her hysterical status. I recalled freaking the hell out when my water broke, mostly because Caleb was late. He didn't want to be born until after my due date. Like any other expecting mother, I put so much emphasis on that day, like it would be *the* big day. When it came and passed, my sense of urgency oddly faded.

The night my water broke, I was crazy. Nervous. Anxious. Worried about doing it alone. Not to mention, going to a freaking vet clinic after hours wasn't the most comforting idea. As my friends and the doula put it, Thank God I didn't need to have a C-section.

"No one does," I confided in her. "With every baby that's born, we're all clueless."

Tessa rushed up. The same with Dante and Romeo. They ran toward us, concerned.

"But it's happening. The baby is coming," Nina told me. "It's seriously happening. Right now!"

She'd stood to put her water glass in the sink and as soon as she was upright, her water broke. I didn't recall it being *that* much liquid, but I supposed the perspective made a difference.

I nodded. "I think it's fair to say—"

She cringed, curling over as she rode out another contraction. Her hand slapped onto my arm and she didn't let go.

"Okay." I winced through her tight grip. "Yeah, these contractions are coming faster."

"Where the hell is Danicia?" Romeo asked.

Dante was at Nina's other side, helping her breathe through the contraction. She gripped his arm too as Tessa ran out of the room, announcing she was grabbing Nina's packed hospital bag to bring.

"Danicia's on vacation," Franco said as he ran inside with Caleb.

Caleb dragged his wide-eyed stare at the puddle on the floor to Nina growling at the pain. "Mom. She made you bleed."

I looked down, pausing in stroking Nina's hair back from her face. Blood seeped out a bit from beneath her nails. She clutched my forearm so hard that her nails cut into my skin.

"It's okay." I shrugged. "It happens." *But oh, my God. Ow, that hurts.*

Dante frowned, trying to talk to her calmly and coach her to breathe through the contraction. When he attempted to move her hand from holding my arm to his, she shook her head.

"No." She shook her head faster. "I want Chloe here. She's helping me."

"Okay. Okay." Dante glanced at me as Franco continued to talk on the phone behind us, arranging transportation to the hospital. "She's here."

I really was. Next to her for support through her baby coming early. One among this closeknit group who welcomed me in their home. And maybe, pending Franco's conversation with Caleb outside, maybe as an actual relative as a Constella Mafia wife soon.

It hit me then. This wasn't a fickle, temporary stay here. This wasn't a vacation or an excuse for protecting me and Caleb.

I was here to *stay*, and I regretted that it'd taken me so long to get here, to learn all that I had and toughen up on my own out there to know that I belonged where my heart was, with Franco.

"I'm not going anywhere," I told her.

"Come with me. Please. Please come with me to the hospital."

I nodded as Dante tried to rub her back and comfort her while Franco spoke with the guards and drivers.

"I will. I'm right here."

"Just breathe—"

"I *am* breathing," she snapped at Dante. As soon as she shouted, she pouted. "I'm sorry. I don't want to yell, but it's not helping. You're not helping. I think you got the breathing things all messed up and I'm scared and panicking, and you're just not helping right now."

He stopped trying to shift her hand from my arm to his. "Okay. That's fine. Yell at me all you want. I won't leave your side."

Both of them were suffering heightened senses of alarm.

"I've got your bag," Tessa said as she ran back into the room.

"But where is Danicia?" Romeo asked again.

It was all commotion, everyone seeming to rush and talk over each other at once. I focused on calming Nina down while we got ready to leave.

"Vacation," Dante replied.

"She thought she could fly to see her niece's graduation with plenty of time before the baby would come." Nina stood, clutching my arm.

"We'll call her," Dante said. "The doctors at the hospital already know her and have been in contact with her throughout your appointments and everything."

Nina nodded, but she still seemed so damn scared. "Please, Chloe. Stay with me."

"I'm right here."

"I'll hang back with Caleb," Franco offered.

"No." Nina shook her head as Dante and I tried to get her toward the door. She waddled, hissing with the contractions that kept coming. "No. I don't want Chloe separated from *her* baby."

"I'm okay with my dad," Caleb piped up.

"No. She's been so scared for so long and so—" She cried out in pain again, but once she caught her breath, walking slower, she shook her head. "No. I don't want you to worry about where Caleb is," she told me.

I looked at Franco, then Tessa and Romeo. Raising my brows, I cleared my throat. "Rule number one. What the pregnant woman giving birth wants, she gets. Am I right?"

"Let's go," Dante ordered. "All of you."

"Yeah. Sure. Right, right." Franco ushered us all to go with Nina. Guards and soldiers came in through the front door, alarmed but alert and ready to act.

"Let's go. Let's go." Franco handled getting us out and into a car. Romeo and Tessa helped get things settled and saw to everyone in the cars and security arranged. While Romeo was on the phone sending guards to the hospital, Tessa and Caleb got into a car. Franco spoke with the men here, dictating a security formation for the trip.

More than once, he glanced at me. He didn't look concerned for me, but Nina.

"There we go. In the back," I coached her.

"The seats—"

"Fuck the seats, Nina," Dante growled. "We'll buy a new damn car."

She panted through another contraction and I frowned. "Time these," I told him. "They'll want to know how close the contractions are coming."

He nodded, grabbing his phone to jot it down.

"And go," I told the driver.

"Go!" Nina echoed as soon as the door was closed.

"Go before I have this baby in the car—ah!"

I winced, wondering whether she could be right. Typically, first babies took a while. First-time moms could be in labor for many hours, even days. She seemed to want to break that rule, rushing straight into labor.

"It's too early. It's too early," she chanted between contractions. "I'm only thirty-seven weeks and one day."

I nodded. "That's doable, Nina. That's not bad. They schedule C-sections at thirty-nine weeks on the dot, and that's just a couple of weeks away."

"Oh, God!" She sobbed between heaving breaths. "What if that happens? What if I have to have a C-section on top of this?"

I shook my head. "Then you have a C-section. It's not that bad. However you bring this baby into the world, it is what it is."

"But I'm so scared."

"No, you're not," I soothed. "You're strong. You've got this. You're just unaware and nervous about the unknown."

She nodded.

"But you're so doing this. You've got this. And you have nothing to fear."

She tightened her hand on my arm through the next contraction.

"Those weren't…" She gasped as the wave passed. "Those weren't Braxton-Hicks."

I laughed weakly. "No, they weren't. And now you know."

"Now I know? What, like I'll do this again and know for the next time. No. Nooo. No. Hell no. I'm never having sex again. Ever, *ever* again."

Dante furrowed his brow, trying to calm her and rub her back as she curled onto me.

"I doubt that."

"No." She shook her head against me. "Never. Not if having a baby feels like a bowling ball is slamming through my hips. I will never have sex again for the rest of my life."

I winced and shot Dante a look over her head. "She doesn't mean that," I mouthed.

He rolled his eyes, staying focused on her.

"Oh, my God. Chloe, I *am* making you bleed." She sat up a bit but was stopped with another contraction.

"It's fine. It's nothing."

"It is not fine. You just accepted the idea of moving and staying with us, with Franco, and now I'm scaring you away, mutilating your arm and oh—"

I gritted my teeth through the ferocity of her grip on me. Her arm shook with the strain of her toughing out the contraction.

"I just can't let go. You've done this. You know how this goes. I really want you to help me through this."

"Whatever you want, Nina. I'm here to help."

It was a mad rush to get to the hospital, but we got there in record time. No baby was born in the backseat, but with how quickly she strained to tough out the contractions, I wasn't sure if they'd get her to a room.

"Nina, let her go." Dante urged Nina to release my arm so I could let the nurses and emergency techs help get her out of the car.

"No." She shook her head, not caring that she'd latched on to me as some sort of grounding presence. "I want Chloe to help me."

"I'm right here," I said as I crawled back out of the car, held back by her hand on my arm. "I'll be right here, but we've got to get you out of the backseat and inside."

"Hold my hand," Dante offered, giving her his other hand.

She sobbed, holding on to me. "I want her to stay with me. You don't understand. I don't understand. I don't have my mom, I don't have a sister. No one. I want *her* with me because she gets it."

I frowned. Half of her tirade sounded like nothing but hysterical nonsense. She wasn't a needy, demanding woman. Not once since I met her had she acted like this. But if she was about to push that baby out, she had every right to act however she wanted to. Maybe she had underlying fears that needed to be addressed, abandonment or whatnot, but now wasn't the time to analyze that.

"Okay, okay." I nodded at Dante, talking to him and the staff trying to get her out of the car. "Dante, you open your door. You back up and get out, and we can get her out from that side of the car. I'll crawl through."

It seemed silly, but it worked. Dante guided her to angle to his door, and once he was out, the techs and nurses teamed up to assist her out of the car. I did just as I said I would, crawling out with her, tethered by her hand on my arm.

"Chloe, please. Can you stay with me?"

I nodded. "Absolutely. I'm here to help," I repeated.

As she was transferred to the gurney, though, she had to release my arm.

"Holy shit," an emergency tech said at the blood dripping down from the crescent shapes of her nails.

"Yeah." I winced. Blood flowed through my arm now that she wasn't holding it so tightly and awkwardly.

"We'll get that wrapped up." He nodded at me as they got Nina situated on the gurney.

Dante went with her, but with all the staff, Constella guards, and others being rushed into the emergency room, it was so chaotic that I felt dizzy for a second.

Franco and Caleb followed after Romeo and Tessa who rushed up from the side parking area.

I sighed at the sight of Caleb running toward me, no doubt excited but shocked by the turn of these events.

"Mom—"

Someone else cut in closer, intercepting him.

I locked my stare on Wes as he wrapped his arm around my son's body.

Caleb fought and wriggled the lanky man who not only was acting insane, but looked it too. His eyes were bloodshot and wide open with a crazed look. He was gaunt and thin, with wild, unkempt hair sticking up. In wrinkled clothes and standing like he was limping, he looked unhinged.

"Let me go!" Caleb jammed his elbow into Wes's stomach.

He grunted in pain, but he didn't release my son. He tightened his arm around him and snuck a gun out from his pocket to press it against his side.

"No!" I shot my arm out to reach for them, to physically slap this asshole from my son.

Panic swept through me. I was already overwhelmed and on edge from this whole morning with Nina and the rush to get her here. But this? Now Wes had to show up and threaten my son?

Franco walked up confidently, his furious gaze on my ex.

No. Not *my* son.

Our son. Terror kept me in a vise, but I tried to steady my breaths with what was different about this time that my ex tried to get into my life and ruin it.

It was Franco's turn to defend *our* son and keep him safe.

"Chloe." Tessa found me, hugging me back.

Romeo strode past us, brushing against me as he reached under his jacket.

"Let them." Tessa nodded, tugging me away. "You don't want to watch. You don't want to see this. Trust me."

"But—" I swallowed hard, unable to just walk away.

"Trust me. They'll handle this." She looked around, noticing the guards flanking them.

I caught Franco's gaze. He stared at me, not trying to hide the utter malice and darkness that he felt at the sight of another man holding our son, threatening him.

He gazed at me, as though searching for an answer.

I nodded, knowing he would be killing this man. All I could do was trust that he wouldn't let Caleb witness the worst of it.

He nodded slightly in reply, turning back to Wes.

"Get your hands off my son," he growled.

31

FRANCO

Seeing someone put their hands on Caleb pissed me off with a fury I'd never fully experienced before.

To dare to point a gun at him?

I don't fucking think so.

I'd faced instances of my family being threatened. Dante under the aim of a gun. Romeo being captured and hit. Liam beat up. Countless others. Even if they weren't blood relations, every single person in the Constella *was* family. *My* family, a representative of someone I'd go to every end of the earth to protect.

But my son? *My son?*

Wes pressing the end of his gun barrel at my son tripped me into a feral rage that I strained to contain.

I did. I tried to mask the pure anger and scorching malice that I wanted to unleash on that man. Caleb was just learning about me. He was already curious about why I—and everyone else at the house—carried guns.

I didn't want him to fear me or what we did. I didn't want to allow a barrier between us as he came to terms with the fact that his father was a trained killer, that I supervised soldiers capable of torturing our enemies and ending the lives of those who crossed us.

For him, to preserve my son's innocence, I contained my wrath the best I could.

"I told you to get your hands off my son. Now."

Wes sneered, heaving deep, spittle-flying breaths as he kept Caleb close. "Your son? He's just a bastard no one wants." He laughed hard once. "No one but those old fuckers. I killed the judge last week. But the old bitch didn't care. She still wants me to bring this bastard to her so she can—"

"No." Caleb wrestled to get away. "You're not taking me anywhere."

"Shut up! Shut up, you little piece of shit." Wes shook him a bit, growling with the effort. "I've spent years wanting you out of the way so I could have my woman."

"My mom's not your girlfriend," Caleb shouted.

"She's mine!" Wes roared. "If she won't come to me and be mine, I'll kill her! She has to be *mine*. I'll order hits on every boss she has. I'll follow her everywhere she goes and prove to her that she has to be with *me*."

Romeo glanced at me, alert and on edge. He was likely making the same conclusions I was.

Wes was crazy. He had to be mentally unstable to act like this, but with his confession, he cleared up the mystery about who shot up the A&J Deli.

I bet Romeo was also thinking that it'd be nice to have Liam here. A sniper shot from a distance, and Wes would be dead.

Already, people were noticing the presence of the Constella men waiting for my order. They spotted Wes foaming at the mouth and acting like a lunatic.

And that wouldn't fly. Not on my watch. Any one of these people near the hospital could call someone to get him and likely have him admitted to the psych ward where he clearly belonged.

Someone could call the cops and have him arrested. Maybe his connections would get him out and free, but that also meant the law enforcement agencies would butt into what was now a very personal matter.

Wes Morrison was a dead man walking, and *I* would be the one who'd have the pleasure of ending his life. All this pent-up rage I tried to contain in the face of the watching public eye, in front of my son, would be spent on ending his life.

Romeo nodded, showing me that he was ready. He was aware that we needed to wrap this up sooner than later. We couldn't risk anyone intervening.

"Let him go." I lifted my hand to tug at my ear, showing Caleb the tell that I'd just shown him this morning when we talked and played basketball.

He didn't flinch or show a sign of fear. He also didn't give away that he saw my tell.

Wes didn't notice, scanning all the soldiers around us.

Then he moved. He growled and lunged for Caleb as he twisted and feinted, just like I'd advised him earlier.

Soldiers parted, letting him sprint toward Chloe and Tessa who stood together behind Romeo and other Constella men.

Wes shot, but he was too slow to hit anyone. The bullet went astray with his lousy aim, but commotion followed anyway. Passersby screamed and ducked for cover. Others shouted to call the police. In the second that Wes fired, the soldiers were on him, taking his gun, restraining him, and bringing him into one of the cars where they'd wait for my order.

After the years of fear and anxiety he'd given Chloe and Caleb, his capture seemed so... anticlimactic. So weak and dull.

Chloe hugged Caleb tightly as they watched Wes get taken away. Even though it was only one gunshot that was fired, security was already rushing from the hospital.

"Go on," I told them. "Keep an eye on your mom for me, okay?"

Caleb nodded, still hugging Chloe. "Okay, Dad. I will."

Dad. My heart was full. It swelled with love and pride. Lurking in my mind, though, darkness grew and intensified.

Chloe caught my eye, and I knew what she had to be thinking. What she had to be feeling. She was well aware that I would kill Wes. She had to know that was coming. With a careful, stern frown, she nodded once, acknowledging it.

She could acknowledge that this was who I was. Not a bad boy her parents disapproved of, but her hero. Her protector. It wouldn't be easy. She'd need to come to terms with this, and we would both need to explain more things to Caleb, but right now, it was time to kill this motherfucker and move on with our lives.

"Go on." Chloe urged Caleb to go inside with Tessa. "I'll be right there."

I stood still, watching her come to me in the parking lot. After she pressed a soft kiss to my lips, she sighed and stared at me. "Be careful."

I smiled. "I always am. Go on. Go help Nina. I'll be back shortly."

A slightly troubled expression covered her face as she backed up, but she nodded. "Thank you, Franco."

I chuckled. "Oh, it's my pleasure, sweetheart."

I turned with Romeo to go to the cars.

"I ordered them to take him to the nearest warehouse."

I nodded as I sat in the backseat with him and closed the door. "Good."

I couldn't wait to kill this bastard. She'd never have to fear him again. It sounded like he'd killed her dad, and I would find a way to handle her mother.

Nothing would ever stand in the way of my future with Chloe and Caleb.

No one would ever dare to pull us apart again.

My heart had always belonged to her. A part of me had already lived on in him.

We were a family, and after I got the satisfaction of removing Wes from this world and getting him out of the picture forever, all would be right in my life. Chloe had come to me and loved me, and she seemed to love me and accept me for the killer I had to be. Caleb had hugged me and called me Dad, already glad to give me his permission to marry his mom.

I smiled, watching the scenery blur out the window, content that finally, at last, my heart was stitched back together and whole.

32

CHLOE

even months later...

"I can't believe the cake turned out this well," I told Dante as we walked past the dessert table at Eva's baby shower.

"All I can say is the next one had better be a boy," the Mafia Boss joked.

I smiled at the princess crown of a cake, commemorating the fact that Eva and Liam would soon be bringing another baby into the family. In the conservatory again, we enjoyed the pool, the food, and the company. Like we often did.

Life was good, and even though I struggled through moments of needing to look the other way when Franco and the others had to act in violence, I knew that they did so to keep us all safe.

"Franco wants to keep ours a surprise," I reminded Dante.

He nodded, chuckling as he got a cupcake and took it to a table. I followed him there, smiling at everyone having fun.

These Mafia men worked hard, but they played hard too.

"It doesn't matter," Dante said as we sat. "But it'd even it out."

"Liv and Sofia," I said, counting Liam's toddler and the sweet baby girl Nina gave birth to just a little earlier than expected.

He pointed at Caleb. "Then we've got Caleb." He gestured at Eva snacking at another table. "They'll have Rose soon."

"And then…" I shrugged, smiling about the baby I carried in my belly. "Who knows?"

Franco and I married shortly after Sofia was born.

Wes was dead. I didn't ask questions. I didn't want to know any details. All I needed to know was that the main threat to my happiness and my son's safety was gone.

He confessed to killing my father, and just a month after Franco proposed, shortly after Wes was removed, they learned that my mother suffered a heart attack and didn't make it. I supposed a life of hatred could predispose someone to have a short lifespan, and I didn't mourn her at all. How could I when she'd tried to have my son killed—twice?

Without any of those worries, I was completely free. I had family, a found family here, as well as the real one with Franco as my husband.

Finished with desserts, Dante sat back and looked out over the room with me. "I don't think I've ever been happier."

"Yeah?" I nodded. "I agree."

"Just over a year ago, all I wanted to do was work and avoid a gold-digger who wanted to latch her claws into me." He gestured at everyone in here. "Now, I'm married. I have a daughter. Daughter-in-law. My niece's family is expanding. Yours is. And Caleb…" He sighed, grinning with complete and utter contentedness.

"I've fucking got it all, Chloe."

"We do." I sat back and marveled at the strong kicks of my baby, so active in my belly.

Caleb and Franco really hit it off. My son adjusted so well to everyone here, but the cutest thing of all was how Dante was such a grandfatherly figure to him. The Mafia Boss was like that with Olivia, too, and we constantly joked how the kids had the patriarch of the entire family wrapped around their little fingers.

He was right, though. We all faced our hardships to get to this day. Danger awaited still, but we'd overcome the threats that tested us all.

Life was good.

And I knew I truly had it all. I always would as long as I had Franco in my life.

As though he knew I was thinking about him, the former bad boy who stole my heart caught my eye. With that cocky smile of his that I loved so much, he winked.

Then and now, he was the other half of my soul. Together again, for good, we would be destined for a long life of nothing but happiness and love.

Printed in Great Britain
by Amazon